"Kayo! They've found us! Here comes the search party!"

The man and Kayo stopped wrestling and turned toward Rosie. For one brief second, while the man looked for the reported search party, he loosened his hold. Instantly, Kayo wrenched herself free and took off.

As soon as Kayo was out of the man's grip, Rosie turned and ran away. She knew Kayo would catch up to her; Kayo was a much faster runner than Rosie was.

The man stared after Kayo for a moment before he realized that Rosie had tricked him. There was no rescue party. There were no people coming through the woods.

He grabbed the lantern and started after the girls. Anger made a muscle in the side of his neck twitch. He would catch those two kids. No sweat.

They were lost, but he knew every tree and bush in these woods for miles in all directions. He could draw a map of this forest with his eyes closed.

There was no way two lost kids could escape from him.

Not here. Not at night.

Books by Peg Kehret

Cages
Horror at the Haunted House
Nightmare Mountain
Sisters, Long Ago
Terror at the Zoo
Frightmares:™ #1: Cat Burglar on the Prowl
Frightmares:™ #2: Bone Breath and the Vandals
Frightmares:™ #3: Don't Go Near Mrs. Tallie
Frightmares:™ #4: Desert Danger
Frightmares:™ #5: The Ghost Followed Us Home
Frightmares:™ #6: Race to Disaster
Frightmares:™ #7: Screaming Eagles

Available from MINSTREL Books

FRIGHTMARES™

Screaming Eagles

Peg Kehret

A MINSTREL® BOOK

PUBLISHED BY POCKET BOOKS

New York   London   Toronto   Sydney   Tokyo   Singapore

This book is a work of fiction. Names, characters, places and incidents are products of the author's imagination or are used fictitiously. Any resemblance to actual events or locales or persons, living or dead, is entirely coincidental.

A MINSTREL PAPERBACK *Original*

 A Minstrel Book published by
POCKET BOOKS, a division of Simon & Schuster Inc.
1230 Avenue of the Americas, New York, NY 10020

Copyright © 1996 by Peg Kehret

ISBN: 1416991069

ISBN: 978-1-4169-9106-9

First Minstrel Books paperback printing May 1996

10 9 8 7 6 5 4 3 2 1

FRIGHTMARES is a trademark of Simon & Schuster Inc.

A MINSTREL BOOK and colophon are registered trademarks of Simon & Schuster Inc.

Cover art by Dan Burr

Printed in the U.S.A.

For Eric Konen

CARE CLUB
We Care About Animals

I. Whereas we, the undersigned, care about our animal friends, we promise to groom them, play with them, and exercise them daily. We will do this for the following animals:

> **WEBSTER** (Rosie's cat)
> **BONE BREATH** (Rosie's dog)
> **HOMER** (Kayo's cat)
> **DIAMOND** (Kayo's cat)

II. Whereas we, the undersigned, care about the well-being of *all* creatures, we promise to do whatever we can to help homeless animals.

III. Care Club will hold official meetings every Thursday afternoon or whenever else there is important business. All Care Club projects will be for the good of the animals.

Signed:

Rosie Saunders

Kayo Benton

Screaming Eagles

Chapter

1

"Don't go too far," Mrs. Saunders warned.

"We won't," Rosie said.

"And stay together," Mrs. Saunders said.

"We will."

"Do you have your whistle?" Mrs. Saunders asked.

"I have it," Rosie's friend, Kayo, said.

"And your water bottles?"

"Mom!" Rosie said. "Quit worrying. We're only going for a bike ride. Nothing bad can happen to us on a simple little bike ride."

"Let's hope not," Mr. Saunders said. "My nerves need a rest."

"No Care Club activity ever turns out to be simple," Mrs. Saunders said.

"This time it will. It's an educational project," Rosie explained as she and Kayo buckled on their bicycle helmets. "Since the bald eagle is America's national emblem, we decided to learn all about eagles. I'm going to write an extra credit report for school about what we learn."

"How can you stand to write an extra report," Kayo said, "when you could spend your time playing baseball?"

"I'd rather write," Rosie said as she gave Bone Breath a dog biscuit to make up for leaving him behind.

The cairn terrier gobbled it in two bites and then wagged his tail eagerly, hoping for more.

"Be careful," Mrs. Saunders called as the girls rode away.

They were on a weekend motor home trip in the North Cascades National Park, and Rosie and Kayo hoped to see some of the bald eagles that nest in the area. That afternoon, Mr. and Mrs. Saunders had parked at a picnic area next to the Skagit River, and now Rosie and Kayo set off on their bicycles.

They pedaled along the two-lane road, stopping once under a tree to eat the cookies they had brought along.

"My mom treats me like a baby sometimes," Rosie complained as she reached for her water bottle.

"All moms do that," Kayo replied. "One night last week, my mother came in my room to say good night, and she asked if I had brushed my teeth."

Rosie smiled. "Had you?" she asked.

"Of course," Kayo said. "I told her I've brushed my teeth every night since I was two, so why does she ask me?"

"What did she say?"

"She asked if I remembered to floss."

"When we go away to college," Rosie said, "we'll probably get letters from our moms reminding us to put on clean underwear every day."

About two miles after their snack, they spotted a narrow gravel road that angled up the hillside.

"It's probably a Forest Service road," Kayo said. "Let's follow it and see where it goes."

"It's too rough for our bikes," Rosie said. "We'll have to walk."

"A hike would be fun. And we're more likely to see eagles farther uphill."

"When we come down, we had better start back, or Mom will worry."

They hid their bikes and helmets behind a clump of bushes, several yards off the side of the main road, and started to climb the gravel road.

The narrow road ended at the top of a high hill.

"I can see why bald eagles almost became extinct," Kayo said as she looked around at the forested foothills. "I would be an endangered species, too, if I had to live in this wilderness."

She lifted the binoculars that hung from a strap around her neck and looked through them. The bare branches of a dead alder tree, like the gnarled hands of an old man, filled the lenses. Kayo fiddled with the focus knob until the branches were clear, and then she aimed higher, looking for eagles.

Rosie did the same with her binoculars, turning her head slowly.

"I see an eagle's nest!" Rosie said.

"Where? Which tree?"

"It isn't in a tree; it's in a crevice at the top of that cliff, on the other side of the ravine."

Kayo looked where Rosie pointed. "You're right," she said. "It's smaller than the nest we saw yesterday in that cottonwood tree, but it's definitely an eagle's nest."

"The biggest eagle nest recorded," Rosie said, "was nine and a half feet across and twenty feet tall. It weighed more than a ton."

Kayo looked at Rosie to see if she was kidding.

"I read about it," Rosie said. "Each year, the eagles build a new nest on top of the old one. Eagles live up to twenty years in the wild, so eventually the nests get huge."

"The one we saw yesterday wasn't that big," Kayo said.

4

"Five feet wide and three feet high is typical," Rosie said.

While Kayo sometimes wished Rosie would spend more time playing catch and less time with her nose in a book, she had to admit Rosie learned a lot of interesting facts by reading.

"Let's sit here awhile and watch the nest," Rosie said as she plopped down on a big boulder. "Maybe an eagle will come to the nest. Besides, my legs are tired from all the riding and climbing."

"Stretch your hamstrings," Kayo said. She stuck one leg out in front of her and, keeping that leg straight, bent over and put her head on her knees and her hands on the ground.

Rosie sat where she was, peering through the binoculars. "I wonder how far we hiked," she said.

"A mile, at least." Kayo finished her leg stretches and sat beside Rosie.

"Most of it," said Rosie, "was straight up."

"It's beautiful up here," Kayo said, "with all the trees around us and the mountains just beyond."

"It's so quiet; I feel as if we should whisper."

"It's more isolated than I expected," Kayo said. "Except for your parents back in the motor home, and any people driving along the road, I'll bet we're the only human beings within thirty miles."

"That's the whole point of coming," Rosie said. "Most eagles won't hunt or nest in areas occupied by humans." She continued to look through her binoculars as she talked, pointing them toward the higher hill across the chasm.

"Kayo!" Rosie's voice was taut. "Look over there."

"What? Do you see an eagle?"

"There's a man climbing the rocks, on the other side of the ravine. He's right below the nest."

Kayo aimed her binoculars in that direction. "I see him," she said.

"He shot that rope over his head with a crossbow," Rosie said. "There's an anchor on the end of the rope; the anchor is stuck in the cliff above him."

"Maybe he's from the state wildlife department. Maybe he's doing a study about eagles."

"If he's from the wildlife department, he would know that eagles want to be left alone. He wouldn't climb near a nest."

"He's probably just one of those people who like the challenge of climbing rocks," Kayo said, "and he doesn't know he's going toward the bald eagle's nest."

As the man neared the nest, two adult eagles

6

flew out of the woods and swooped toward him. Their white heads and tails, their dark brown bodies, and their yellow feet stood out clearly against the blue sky.

Both girls stood and stepped closer to the edge of the ravine, with their binoculars aimed at the eagles.

"They're beautiful," Rosie said. A tingle climbed her backbone as she watched the magnificent birds.

"They're huge," Kayo said. "I knew eagles have a wing span of six to eight feet, but I didn't realize how wide that is compared to a person."

The eagles screamed at the man, their shrill screeches echoing across the valley. *Kak! Kak! Kak!*

"The man must realize there's a nest," Kayo said. "Those eagles are screaming at him to get away."

The man paused and looked up at the eagles.

"He sees them," Kayo said.

"He sees the nest, too. Why doesn't he go back down?"

The girls peered silently for a minute. The climber braced his feet against the cliff and held on to the rope with one hand. With the other hand, he pulled thick gloves from his backpack. He also removed a mesh bag, which he clipped to his belt. He put the gloves on and continued the climb.

"There are baby birds in the nest," Kayo said. "The tops of their heads are poking up."

"Two of them," Rosie agreed. "They probably hear their parents screaming, and they want to see what's going on."

The girls watched in growing dismay as the man continued toward the nest, with the eagles circling and screeching above him.

Kak! Kak!

"He's going to the nest on purpose," Kayo said.

An eagle dropped straight down at the man, talons extended. The man leaned into the cliff, flattening his back against the rock. One hand grasped the rope and moved it from side to side, making a moving barrier between his body and the attacking eagle.

The eagle veered away from the rope, flew up to the top of the cliff, and landed. It sat directly above the nest, looking down. The second eagle continued to circle overhead, still screaming.

When the man was high enough to see into the nest, he put one shoulder against the cliff and grasped the rope with one hand. With the other hand, he reached toward the nest.

"Oh!" Rosie gasped as the man's hand dipped over the edge of the nest. "Look!"

"Oh!" Kayo echoed. "He's taking a baby eagle!"

Chapter

2

The color drained from Rosie's face as she watched.

The man's gloved hand lifted an eaglet from the nest and stuffed it quickly into the mesh bag.

The eaglet's feathers were all brown. It flapped its small wings against the mesh.

The adult eagle that had been circling overhead dove toward the man. Its talons reached toward the mesh bag.

The man jerked his head out so that the eagle's talons struck his helmet. The eagle screamed, flew upward, and continued circling. The other eagle flew to the nest and stood over the second eaglet.

"This is horrible," Kayo said. She pulled her shirt collar up, as if by keeping the cold wind off her neck she could also keep the cold facts of what she saw out of her mind. "That baby eagle will probably die without its parents to take care of it."

With the eaglet struggling helplessly in the bag, the man descended the cliff. Going up, he had felt for handholds in the rock crevices and pulled himself up a few feet at a time. Going down, he grasped the rope. Using his feet only to keep his body from slamming into the side of the cliff, he let his hands slide swiftly down the rope.

Rosie dropped her binoculars, letting them hang by the strap around her neck. She grabbed her vocabulary notebook and pencil from her pocket. "Describe him to me," she said. "I'll write it down so we are accurate when we report him."

"Red shirt," Kayo said. "Make that a red plaid shirt. White helmet. It looks like the hard hats that construction workers wear. He has long hair that hangs out below the hat."

Rosie wrote quickly.

"Jeans," Kayo said. "Tan climbing boots. He has a beard. I can't see his face now, only the back of his head, but I saw the beard earlier, when he was putting the gloves on. The gloves are gray, with wide cuffs that extend halfway up his arm."

Rosie wrote quickly, abbreviating some of the words.

"He looks like a large man," Kayo continued. "Six feet tall, or maybe six-two. He must be strong, to be able to climb that cliff."

As she talked, Kayo followed the man's descent by lowering the wide end of her binoculars. "The big eagles keep swooping down," she reported. "The man is nearing the bottom of the cliff, but the eagles are still trying to rescue their baby."

Rosie brushed a tear from her cheek. "Why would anyone do such a mean thing?" she said. "Bald eagles are so beautiful. And so many people have worked to save them from extinction."

Rosie stuffed her notebook in her pocket and put the binoculars back to her eyes just in time to see the man reach the bottom of the cliff. "Let's try to see where he goes," she said. "He probably has a four-wheel-drive vehicle; maybe we can get a description of it."

The man did something to a clasp on his rope and then yanked on the rope. The rope and anchor tumbled to the ground, landing at his feet. He wound the rope loosely into a circle, picked up the crossbow, and strode quickly along the base of the cliff, toward a thick stand of trees.

The girls hurried in the same direction, away from the gravel road, following him through their binoculars.

"I can see his face now," Rosie said. "He looks

like pictures in a history book, like one of the early settlers."

The adult eagles flew overhead, still screaming. They took turns diving toward the man.

The baby eagle flapped and struggled to get out of the mesh bag.

Once the man grasped his rope about six feet below the anchor and swung the anchor around and around. It whizzed over his head, scaring off the big eagles.

Kayo and Rosie stumbled through low bushes and tall ferns, keeping their binoculars focused on the man.

"He's going into the forest," Rosie said.

"I can still see his red shirt through the trees," Kayo said. She pushed on through the bushes. They were thicker now, with trees interspersed, but Kayo and Rosie kept going. An occasional glimpse of the shirt told them they were traveling in the same direction the man was going.

Soon there were more trees, and the terrain sloped downward. The girls had trouble keeping their footing.

Fifteen minutes after the man with the eaglet went into the forest, Rosie's foot slipped, and she had to drop the binoculars and grasp a tree branch to keep from falling. "I can't see where I'm going and watch for the man at the same time," she said.

"Have you seen him in the last couple of minutes?" Kayo asked.

"No. We've lost him. He's gone too deep into the woods." She looked up. "I don't see the big eagles anymore, either," she said. "And I don't hear them screaming."

"Maybe they went back to the nest to take care of their other baby. Eagles usually hatch only one or two eggs; I'm glad this pair hatched two."

"Do you realize," Rosie said, "that we witnessed a crime? Bald eagles are a protected bird."

"It's against the law to kill or injure them, but he didn't actually hurt it. Is it against the law to take a baby bird away from its parents?"

"It's illegal to harass them or to possess a bald eagle's egg or even to take part of a nest."

"We need to get to a telephone," Kayo said. "We have to report this to the park ranger or the wildlife department. Maybe they can catch the man and get the eaglet back before it's too late."

"It will not be easy to find a telephone in the middle of nowhere," Rosie said. "By the time we hike back down the gravel road and ride our bikes to the motor home, that man will be gone for good. And so will the baby eagle."

"Your mother was right," Kayo said. "No Care Club project is ever simple." She turned and began climbing uphill, the way they had come.

13

Rosie hesitated. "Maybe we could take a short-cut," she said.

"How?"

"Instead of going straight back, we can angle to our right. When we find the gravel road, we'll be partway down it."

The girls plunged into the woods.

The dense underbrush made walking difficult. From a distance, the forest looked as if it consisted entirely of tall trees. Western red cedar and Douglas fir trees stayed green all year; their branches, with soft new growth at the tips, brushed easily aside. The alder and vine maples had dropped their leaves in the fall. Winter snow packed the fallen leaves together, creating a soft brown carpet underfoot. Now, in early May, fresh leaves covered the branches again, creating green canopies overhead.

Beneath these large trees, thickets of huckleberry bushes, Oregon grape, and other low-growing shrubs slowed the girls' progress. Several times, Rosie and Kayo had to move left or right in order to get past tall, thorny stalks of devil's club. They went between waist-high sword ferns and stepped over nurse logs—fallen, rotting trees with new trees sprouted on top of them.

"Maybe we should have gone back the way we came," Rosie said. "We aren't going very fast."

14

"It's still shorter this way," Kayo said. "We'll save time."

Kayo led the way, often holding a tree limb back so that Rosie could pass with her. Because Kayo ran every day and lifted weights, she was able to stomp through the undergrowth, raising her knees high, without tiring. Rosie, who spent most of her spare time either reading or playing with Bone Breath and Webster, her dog and cat, puffed along behind.

"Shouldn't we have come to the gravel road by now?" Rosie asked.

"We'll probably be nearly at the bottom when we find it."

Rosie took off her jacket and tied it around her waist. Five minutes later, she put it back on. She was warm from struggling through the woods, but without the jacket, the branches scratched her arms.

Kayo stopped walking and turned to Rosie. "We've come this way before," she said.

"What? You mean we've walked in a circle?" Alarmed, Rosie looked around. "How can you tell?" she asked.

"This big stump, with the moss on it," Kayo said. "We passed it once before."

"Are you sure it's the same stump? I've seen lots of stumps."

"When we went by this one, I tore off a little

piece of moss. I like the way moss feels when I rub it between my fingers." She took a small piece of moss from her pocket and laid it on top of the stump. It fit into the jagged edge of the remaining moss like the last piece of a jigsaw puzzle.

The full meaning of what Kayo had said hit Rosie. "If we walked in a circle," she said, "it means we don't know which way to go. We're lost."

Her last two words lingered in the air as if a cartoonist had drawn a loopy circle around them and floated the circle from Rosie's lips. *We're lost.*

Rosie waited for Kayo to deny it, but Kayo merely nodded her head miserably and stared at Rosie with wide, frightened eyes.

Rosie remembered the map her dad had laid on the kitchen table, when they were planning this trip.

"Look at all that undeveloped space," Mr. Saunders had said. "The North Cascades National Park is surrounded by national forestland. The wilderness goes on and on. No people. No traffic. No television. Only wild animals and gorgeous scenery."

"Peace and quiet," Mrs. Saunders said.

"And bald eagles," Rosie added.

The words, spoken with happy anticipation,

seemed frightening now as Rosie remembered them.

A huge wilderness with no people had sounded wonderful when she was safe in her own kitchen. A wilderness with no people was terrifying when she was somewhere in the middle of it and didn't know how to get out.

"We're lost," Rosie repeated. She sat down on the mossy stump, fighting back panic.

Chapter

3

Tweet! The shrill sound made Rosie jump.

Kayo blew the whistle again. *Tweet! Tweet!*

Ever since Rosie and Kayo were kidnapped in the desert, Mrs. Saunders insisted that one of the girls wear a whistle around her neck whenever they left the motor home. "If you need help," she said, "blow the whistle. Keep blowing until someone hears it."

At the time, Rosie had thought her mother was overprotective and worried about nothing. Now, as she listened to the piercing screech, she was glad Kayo had the whistle.

After Kayo blew the whistle, the girls listened, hoping for a reply. All they heard was a blue jay cawing its anger at their loud noise.

After six attempts, Kayo let the whistle drop back to her chest. "No one hears it," she said. "We're too far away."

"The smart thing to do is wait where we are," Rosie said. "When we don't return to the motor home, Mom and Dad will look for us. If we keep walking, we may go even farther from the road."

"I'm sorry I led us the wrong way," Kayo said.

"It isn't your fault. I'm the one who suggested we take a shortcut."

"We would have been okay if we could have kept walking in a straight line."

The girls sat together on the mossy stump.

"I wonder what the man plans to do with the eaglet," Kayo said.

"Raise it and keep it as a pet?" Rosie suggested. "Some people want exotic pets."

"It's cruel to take a wild animal and keep it confined," Kayo said. "If he wants a pet, let him go to an animal shelter and adopt a dog or a cat."

"Maybe he's going to sell the eaglet. Maybe there's some kind of black market for wild birds."

"It makes me sick even to think about it," Kayo said. She stood up. "I can't just sit here," she said. "I'm going to try to retrace our steps. We broke some branches as we pushed through; maybe I can find my way back to where we started." She slipped the cord with the whistle on it over her head and offered it to Rosie. "You keep this," she said.

"I'm coming with you," Rosie said.

"Are you sure? You can stay here, and if I find my way, I'll send help. Blow your whistle every few minutes."

Rosie shook her head. "If I'm going to be lost in the woods," she said, "I'd rather be lost with you than sit here all alone and wait for someone to find me."

Kayo walked briskly, pushing her way through the undergrowth. Twice she stopped and looked around, hoping to recognize something, anything, that would help to orient her. I should have left marks, she thought, to show which way we went.

Once, on an overnight camping trip with her church youth group, the leader had given each person strips of red ribbon and told them to tie the ribbons on tree branches, to be sure they could always find their way back to camp.

When you really get lost, Kayo thought, you aren't likely to have a pocket full of red ribbons. But I should have used some other kind of marker.

Rosie slapped the back of her neck and then looked at a small smear of blood on her hand. "There are mosquitoes in the woods," she said. "I just got bit."

Instead of answering, Kayo gave another blast on the whistle.

Again, there was no response.

"All these trees muffle the sound," Kayo said.

She picked up a stone the size of a grapefruit and wedged it in the space where a low branch of an elm tree met the trunk.

"What are you doing?" Rosie asked.

"Marking where we've been. If anyone comes looking for us, they'll see stones in the trees and realize we put them there as clues."

"Or we'll find the stones ourselves," Rosie said, "if we go in a circle again."

Kayo pressed on, stopping every few yards to balance a stone on a tree limb.

Rosie batted another mosquito off her cheek. "Mosquitoes always come to me," she complained. "It's as if I had a sign pinned on my back that says, *Free Meal. All Mosquitoes Welcome.*"

Three stones later, while Kayo positioned their clue, Rosie leaned against the base of a pine tree whose branches didn't start until ten feet up. The scent of pine pitch filled her head. It smells like Christmas, she thought.

Memories of decorating a tree, frosting gingerbread men, wrapping presents, and keeping secrets filled Rosie's head. They were happy memories, but they brought tears to Rosie's eyes. We're in big trouble, she thought. We could be lost for days. Weeks! We might never be found. I might never see Mom and Dad again, or Bone Breath and Webster. My brother will come home from college next month, and I'll be gone. I might never have another Christmas.

The possibilities were too awful to think about; Rosie pushed them out of her mind.

Kayo finished balancing the rock on a big branch. She turned to Rosie with her finger to her lips, signaling Rosie to be quiet.

Rosie stood still. She looked and listened. If Kayo had heard voices in the distance, she wouldn't want Rosie to be quiet; Kayo would shout for help. So what had she heard, or seen? An elk? A bear? A bobcat? The wilderness was home to many wild animals, Rosie knew. What would one of them do if it suddenly came upon two girls?

And then Rosie heard it, too. It was a rustling sound in the trees, off to her left. She moved toward Kayo, careful not to make any sound.

They waited.

The rustling came closer. Small branches snapped.

Rosie leaned close to Kayo and whispered in her ear. "Maybe we should yell or blow the whistle."

Kayo whispered back, "If it's people looking for us, they would be yelling themselves. If it's not people . . ."

She didn't finish the sentence, but Rosie knew

what she meant. *If it's not people, we don't want whatever it is to know we're here.*

Kayo inched silently to the other side of the pine tree, away from the rustling sound. Rosie did the same.

The girls stood close together, peeking out from behind the tree trunk. They heard a chewing sound. Whatever was there was eating something.

Kayo's eyes scanned the forest. It was nearly dusk, she realized. It gets dark early in the woods, where the trees reach high to block out the sunlight.

The rustling came again. As the girls stared in that direction, a mule deer stepped into view, a beautiful brown doe.

Rosie and Kayo sagged against the tree trunk with relief.

The doe stopped and looked toward the pine tree. Her large ears twitched. She moved her head slowly, gazing both left and right. She stretched her neck up and nibbled leaves off a wild crabapple tree, crunching them noisily. When she finished chewing, she stared at the pine tree again, standing as still as one of those deer statues that people sometimes put on their lawns. Then she turned and, with a flick of her black and white tail, leaped gracefully over a four-foot-high huckleberry bush and disappeared into the woods.

Kayo and Rosie smiled at each other as they came out from behind the tree.

"She was so pretty," Rosie said. "I wonder if she saw us, or smelled us."

"My grandma says that when life looks bleak, it may be a blessing in disguise," Kayo said. "I never saw a deer up close before, so maybe getting lost is a blessing in disguise."

Rosie looked at Kayo as if her hair had turned purple. Deer or no deer, how could Kayo possibly feel it was good to be lost?

I don't want my blessings wearing costumes, Rosie thought. I could enjoy seeing the deer a lot more if we weren't lost in the woods, with no assurance that we'll ever find our way out.

"The sun's going down," Kayo said. Her voice sounded higher than usual, and Rosie realized that the talk about a blessing in disguise had been Kayo's way of trying not to panic. Sort of like whistling in the dark.

Chapter

4

$\mathcal{A}$fter the sun sets," Rosie said, "it will get cold. Maybe we should quit walking and try to build some kind of shelter."

"We'll stay warmer if we keep moving," Kayo said. "Let's keep going until it's dark. We can always cover ourselves with leaves or pine branches if we have to."

The approaching sunset gave a new urgency to their legs, and they walked faster, pushing recklessly through the brush without caring if their clothing snagged.

"I'm hungry," Kayo said.

"So am I."

Rosie swatted her wrist. "So are the mosquitoes."

"That's another reason to keep moving," Kayo said. "They'll bite us even worse if we sit still."

"Maybe we'll find some edible berries," Rosie

said. "Mom and I picked wild huckleberries once. It took us about an hour to pick enough to make a dozen muffins. We had planned to make a huckleberry pie, but it would have taken half a day to get enough berries for that."

"Don't talk about pies and muffins," Kayo said, "or I'll start drooling the way Bone Breath does."

They walked on for a few minutes. While Kayo put another stone in a tree, Rosie said, "Do the woods seem thicker now than they were before? I feel as if there are more trees and more undergrowth than when we first started walking."

"Maybe they only seem thicker because we're getting tired, or because the daylight is fading. It's gloomy, isn't it?"

Rosie nodded. "I'm glad we stayed together. I wouldn't want to be here by myself."

The girls trudged on, no longer confident that they would find the road, but unwilling to sit still and get cold and wait for the mosquitoes to bite.

Rosie's shoelace snagged on a fallen branch and came untied. "Wait a second," she said. "I have to tie my shoe." She put her foot on top of a large rock and quickly retied the shoelace.

"Look!"

Rosie looked where Kayo was pointing. Three

wild blueberry bushes crouched at the edge of a small meadow.

"Dinner!" Kayo cried. She hurried toward the bushes with Rosie at her heels.

"They aren't ripe," Rosie said.

Kayo plucked several of the small green berries from the first bush and popped them in her mouth. She puckered her lips. "Yuck!" she said. She spit the berries on the ground.

"Blueberries are supposed to turn blue before you eat them," Rosie said.

A twig snapped behind them. Both girls turned, hoping to see another deer. A rustling sound came from the woods; another branch snapped.

Rosie and Kayo stood quietly, looking in the direction of the movement. The sounds came closer, approaching the girls.

The snapping noises were louder than when the doe came, and the rustling was less subtle. Perhaps it's more than one deer, Rosie thought. Maybe a whole herd of deer will come to graze in the little meadow at dusk.

The girls waited without moving or speaking.

Crack. Another branch broke, but it sounded bigger than the others. Much bigger.

Kayo and Rosie looked at each other apprehensively, each thinking the same thing. What if it wasn't a deer?

The deer had moved gracefully and quietly;

these noises sounded more like a large, clumsy person in sturdy boots, stomping his way through the woods without making any attempt to be quiet.

Fifteen feet from where the girls stood, the brush moved; Rosie and Kayo glimpsed a broad expanse of dark brown fur. The fur was not smooth, as the deer's had been. It was shaggy. Whatever was coming, it was enormous, and it had coarse, thick fur.

Kayo stiffened and clutched Rosie's sleeve.

Rosie shrank back against the blueberry bushes.

More twigs snapped and scattered as a small shrub was flattened by a gigantic paw with long, sharp claws.

Rosie's heart hammered in her chest.

Kayo took a deep breath and prepared to run.

Both girls fought back panic as a full-grown grizzly bear broke through the brush and headed toward them.

The bear's nose skimmed the ground. He made an occasional snuffling sound as he walked.

The bear ambled over to the rock where Rosie had tied her shoe. He sniffed around the bottom of the rock.

Does he smell me? Rosie wondered. Five minutes ago, I stood beside that rock. I put my foot on it while I tied my shoelace. Does the scent make him think I'm food?

The bear placed one front paw on the rock, which was a foot high and two feet wide. The bear pushed the rock aside as easily as if it had been made of Styrofoam.

Despite her fear, an electric thrill ran down Rosie's arms, making her skin prickle. She glanced at Kayo. Kayo's open mouth clearly showed her awe at such power—and her wide eyes conveyed her fear of what that power could do, if it chose, to two twelve-year-olds.

The bear ate something that had been under the rock.

Rosie wondered what could fit under a big rock. Ants? Beetles? Neither of those seemed large enough for a grizzly bear to bother with.

For several seconds, the bear's tongue licked eagerly at the ground where the rock had been.

The bear, apparently having eaten all of whatever had been hidden under the rock, started toward the girls again. This time, he saw them.

He stopped abruptly and blinked. His ears moved.

Rosie wondered whether the bear had ever seen humans before. If the bear is hungry enough to eat ants, she thought, we must look like Thanksgiving dinner.

Kayo glanced around, searching for a way to

escape. There was no use running across the meadow; even though grizzly bears are large, Kayo knew from watching nature films on TV that they can run with lightning speed.

With all these trees around us, Kayo thought, there should be one we can climb. But trees in a dense forest don't have many sturdy branches down low, because they get sunlight only higher up. The trees the girls could reach quickly had spindly leafless branches or no branches at all for the first ten or twelve feet. There were no footholds. Besides, she told herself, can't bears climb trees?

Kayo's fear increased as she quickly eliminated each escape option as fast as she thought of it.

While Kayo tried to think how to get away, Rosie's mind raced, too, trying to recall what she had read about bears in the free newspaper she had picked up in the North Cascades Visitor Center. Most of the article had dealt with proper cooking and food storage techniques so that people would not attract bears to their campsites.

At the time she had read the newspaper, Rosie thought the most interesting part about bears was the statement that bears are not the most dangerous animals in the wilderness. Humans are.

He's so big, Rosie thought. Or is it a female?

A mother bear, protecting her cubs, might attack a human without any provocation.

Rosie stared at the bear's large paws. Long claws curved downward over the front of the fur on each foot. With all that power behind them, Rosie thought, those claws would cut through a person like ten freshly sharpened butcher knives.

Chapter

5

The bear blinked again and took a step backward.

"I think he's just as scared as we are," Kayo whispered.

That remark made Rosie remember what else the article had said. It stated that if a bear came close to your campsite, you might be able to frighten it away by shouting and banging on pots and pans.

"Blow the whistle," Rosie said.

Kayo looked unsure. What if the sudden noise startled the bear and caused him to attack them?

"Blow it!" Rosie insisted.

As Kayo lifted the whistle to her lips, the bear rocked slightly from side to side as if he were trying to decide which way to go.

"Go away!" Rosie yelled. "Get out of here!"

Tweet! Kayo blew as hard as she could, inhaled quickly, and blew again. *Tweet! Tweet!*

While Kayo blew the whistle, Rosie waved her arms at the bear. "Shoo!" she shrieked. "Shoo! Go away!"

The bear made his move at the second shrill blast of the whistle. He turned and, glancing once over his shoulder at the noisy girls, crashed through the bushes away from them.

The girls listened to the sounds of branches breaking as the bear ran off.

Kayo realized her hands were shaking. "How did you know he'd run away if we made noise?" she asked. "I was afraid it would make him attack us."

"I read an article about bears in that newspaper from the Forest Service."

Kayo had intended to read that newspaper and all the other literature about the wilderness area that Rosie and her parents had gathered, but she never got around to it. While Rosie read, Kayo had spread her beach towel on the ground and had done sit-ups, leg lifts, and biceps curls.

The girls waited a few moments, until they could no longer hear the sounds of the bear's retreat.

Then they walked in the opposite direction from where the bear had gone. Dusk settled over the forest, bringing with it a damp cold.

The girls' spirits sank with the setting sun.

"Mom and Dad will be looking for us by now," Rosie said. "They'll drive the motor home along the road, the direction we were headed. Maybe they'll spot our bikes."

"I wish we had not hidden them so carefully behind those bushes."

"If they don't find the bikes, they'll notify the authorities that we're missing." She thought a moment. "Actually," she said, "they'll notify the authorities if they *do* find our bikes, too."

"Maybe a search-and-rescue team will look for us," Kayo said. "Maybe the governor will call out the National Guard."

Rosie swatted another mosquito from her face. "Whoever finds us," she said, "I hope they bring mosquito repellent."

Five minutes later, Kayo stopped walking and pointed into the trees. "Look," she said. Her voice vibrated with excitement. "Over there."

"What? I don't see anything."

"That dark area, just beyond those next trees. I think it's a roof."

Rosie wrinkled her nose and pushed on her glasses frames, holding the lenses tight against her cheeks. "It is a roof!" she said. "I see a chimney." Relief made her speak louder than usual.

The girls hurried toward the building.

"It's an old log cabin," Kayo said as she pushed aside the branches of a large cedar tree.

The weathered gray-brown logs and the moss-covered roof blended so well with the surrounding forest that the girls had almost missed the cabin. Encircled as it was by thick shrubs and trees, only the roof line was visible, even though Rosie and Kayo were less than twenty feet away.

"Maybe someone lives there," Kayo said. "Maybe there'll be a telephone."

Rosie started to point out that there were no telephone lines in the middle of the forest, but then it occurred to her that the occupants of the log cabin might have a cellular phone.

Both girls hurried through the brush toward the cabin. As they got closer, they saw a single window on the side of the cabin; it was as dark inside the structure as it was in the woods.

That doesn't mean the cabin is unoccupied, Kayo thought. Maybe the owner uses kerosene lamps and hasn't lit them yet. Maybe the owner is asleep.

They were only a few feet from the side of the cabin when Rosie stopped. "Wait," she whispered. "We need to think about this."

"What is there to think about? Somebody might live here. They can help us. And if no one is here, at least it gives us a place to spend the night, where we're safe from bears and who knows what else. There may even be food inside."

"What kind of person would live way out here in the forest?" Rosie said.

"Someone who loves Nature and can't stand cities," Kayo replied. "Or maybe it's a hunting cabin that's only used occasionally."

"There's no hunting allowed in the national park," Rosie said.

"We may not be in the national park any longer. We've walked a long way, and we weren't very far inside the boundary to begin with." Kayo walked faster as she neared the cabin. "Maybe it belongs to an artist who comes here to paint pictures of the wildlife," she said.

"Or maybe," Rosie said, "the occupant is hiding from the law. Maybe it's an escaped prisoner."

"You read too many mystery novels," Kayo said. She emerged from the bushes and walked along the side of the cabin to the front.

A footpath led from the front porch across a small clearing. A large rock squatted in the clearing. As the girls passed the rock, they saw something flat spread on it.

"Maybe that's how he dries his clothes," Rosie whispered.

"It's furry," Kayo said. She looked closer. "It's a squirrel skin," she said.

Two steps led up to a porch that ran across the

full width of the cabin. A rocking chair made of willow branches sat to the right of the door. The chair did not appear sturdy enough to hold a person. A crudely made broom leaned against the wall, and a rusty bucket lay tipped on its side on the bottom step.

Kayo went up the steps, which proved to be as rickety as the chair. There was no doorbell or knocker, so she made a fist and tapped on the door.

"Wait for me," Rosie said, and she bounded up the steps to stand beside Kayo. If there was an escaped convict or some other dangerous person in the cabin, she and Kayo would face him or her together.

"Hello?" Kayo called. "Is anyone here?"

Rosie kept her body half turned toward the woods behind them, ready to flee. She couldn't explain why, but the cabin gave her a bad feeling, as if it held danger within its unpainted walls.

Kayo knocked again and again. When there was no answer, she lifted the wooden latch. "I'm going in," she said.

The wooden latch creaked loudly as she raised it. She pushed the door open a few inches. Both girls peered through the crack, but it was darker inside than out. They could make out only vague shapes.

"Maybe we can find matches and start a fire

in the fireplace," Rosie said. "That would give us light and keep us warm, too."

"How do you know there's a fireplace?" Kayo asked.

"We saw a chimney."

Together, the girls gave the heavy door a shove. It squeaked slowly open.

"Hello?" Rosie said.

When there was still no answer, the girls stepped over the threshold into the dark interior.

"You go right; I'll go left," Rosie said. She put one hand on the log wall, feeling for a source of light.

Kayo did the same, going in the other direction.

Both girls immediately bumped into large pieces of furniture. Rosie's knee hit the end of a bed; Kayo's hands felt a crudely made set of shelves.

"Stand still a minute," Kayo said. "My eyes are getting used to the dark. Look at that table in front of me."

Rosie could make out shapes now, too. A long wooden table stretched almost the full length of the cabin, from the fireplace to the shelves beside Kayo. Large birds formed a line down the center of the table.

"Are they real?" Kayo said. "Or carved?" She stepped closer to the table.

Rosie did the same. "It looks like the displays in a museum," she said. She stopped next to a pintail duck. Reaching out slowly, she touched the duck's feathers. "They're real birds that have been stuffed," Rosie said. She walked slowly along the front of the table. "There's a falcon and a mallard duck and some other kind of duck with a white head."

Kayo walked on the other side of the table, next to the wall. "This one is a spotted owl," Kayo said.

"They are nearly extinct," Rosie said.

The girls moved cautiously along the edge of the table, bending close to the stuffed birds in order to see them clearly.

"The cabin must belong to a taxidermist," Rosie said. "I wonder how he gets all these birds. I suppose an occasional duck dies from a gunshot and the hunter doesn't find the duck, but there are so many different species here. How would he get a falcon? Or a spotted owl?"

"The same way he gets bald eagles," Kayo said. "Here are two adult eagles and an eaglet that was too young to have its white feathers yet."

Rosie shuddered. "This explains why that man stole the baby eagle out of the nest," she said. "This is his cabin."

Kayo got a sick feeling in her stomach. "He took the eaglet so he could kill it and stuff it," she said. She thought of the adult eagles, majestic against the blue sky. The eaglet would have grown to be a beautiful bird, too. It might have fished for salmon, and built a nest of its own, and soared high above the trees for twenty years. Kayo clenched her fists angrily. "What a rotten thing to do," she said.

"He probably sells them," Rosie said. "And he wants different sizes and types of birds. Someone who buys a stuffed adult eagle might also want the eaglet to go with it."

"That's horrible." Kayo moved around the end of the table to a second, smaller table. It wasn't a real table; it was a thick plank resting on two sawhorses. The flat surface contained tools, knives, several skins from small animals, and a metal pie plate filled with what seemed to be marbles. Kayo picked one up and looked closely. "Oh!" she said, and dropped it back in the pie plate.

"What's the matter?"

"There's a whole plate of eyeballs."

"Real ones?" Rosie said. Her voice quavered.

Kayo bent over the pie plate, looking closely at its contents. "Maybe they're glass eyes," Kayo said. "I'm not touching them again to find out."

"This place gives me the creeps," Rosie said.

"I don't want to stay here all night. I'd rather take my chances with the bears."

Kayo did not reply.

Rosie looked at her friend. "What about you?" Rosie said. "Do you want to stay in here?"

Kayo stared past Rosie, toward the open door. "Someone's coming," she said.

Chapter

*R*osie turned and looked behind her out the open door.

A light bobbed in the forest, coming closer. Someone with a flashlight or lantern was walking directly toward the cabin.

Apprehension poured over Rosie. If the light was carried by someone looking for Rosie and Kayo, that person would be calling their names. This person was not. This person was merely walking through the woods toward a cabin, as if that cabin belonged to him.

"Let's go out on the porch," Rosie said. "If it's him, he may not like to find us inside." She ran toward the open door. Kayo hurried around the table and went after her.

Together, the girls stepped from inside the cabin to the porch, pulling the door shut behind them. The door creaked, and the light swung suddenly upward.

They saw that it was an old blue kerosene lantern with a handle. The hand holding the lantern was raised shoulder high, allowing the person to see the girls.

The light also revealed the face of the man who held the lantern. He had shoulder-length hair and a beard so full that it was impossible to tell where the beard ended and his hair began. His face was lined and weathered-looking, as if he spent a lot of time outdoors. If he had worn a fringed leather jacket, he would have looked like an early frontiersman. He wore a red plaid shirt.

Kayo knew it was the same shirt she had described to Rosie as she peered through her binoculars at the eagles' nest. She felt for Rosie's hand and clasped it. Rosie squeezed back.

"Hello," Rosie said.

The man's dark eyes flashed angrily as he strode toward the girls, still holding the lantern aloft.

"You were in my house," he said.

"We're lost," Rosie said. "We found your cabin accidentally, and we hoped you might have a telephone."

"Don't believe in telephones," the man said. He stopped at the foot of the porch steps and glowered up at the girls.

"Do you have a car?" Kayo asked. "Can you give us a ride to town?"

"Don't believe in cars," the man said. "Gasoline pollutes the air."

"You're right about that," Rosie said. "How do you get supplies? Do you walk to town? Are we close enough to walk?"

"Town!" The man spit into the dirt. "Don't go to town. Don't need supplies."

Kayo and Rosie glanced at each other. "Not ever?" Rosie asked.

"Nothing in town but people."

Rosie half expected him to say he didn't believe in people.

"What about water?" Kayo asked. "Where do you get water?"

"Well. Dug the well myself with my pick and shovel. Thirty feet, straight down."

Curiosity overcame Rosie's nervousness. "How did you know where to dig?" she asked.

"Divining rod." A small, satisfied smile curved the corners of his mouth. "Found me a divining rod in the woods and walked around with it until the stick dipped, and then I started digging. There was the water, right where the stick said it would be."

Rosie remembered reading about divining rods. They were just ordinary tree branches, shaped like a Y. The person doing the divining, or dowsing as it was sometimes called, holds on to the tips of the Y, with the long part pointed out in front of him. He walks slowly around, and supposedly the tail of the twig dips down when it passes over water.

"Water witch," Rosie said, remembering the other name for someone who dowses.

The smile vanished from the man's face. "Not a witch," he said. "A dowser."

Kayo jabbed Rosie in the ribs with her elbow.

"Sorry," Rosie said. "I didn't mean you are a witch; I just meant someone I read about."

There was a moment of uneasy silence while the two girls and the unkempt man stared at each other.

Kayo said, "Can you lead us out of here? You wouldn't have to go all the way to town with us, just take us far enough that we'll be able to find our way back to the road."

The man thought for a moment and then shook his head. "Can't leave," he said.

"Could you tell us which direction we should walk?" Rosie said. "We're all turned around. We've been lost for several hours."

"Can't leave," the man repeated.

"I don't suppose you have an extra lantern we could borrow," Kayo said, "or a flashlight. We would bring it back."

"No!"

45

The girls looked at each other. "Then I guess we'll be on our way," Rosie said. "Thanks anyway." She moved across the porch toward the steps. Kayo did the same.

Immediately, the man stepped closer, blocking their way.

"*You* can't leave," the man said.

"What?" Kayo said.

"We have to," Rosie said. "We need to get back to the main road. My parents are frantic by now. Is there any kind of a trail or path leading from your cabin out of the woods?"

"And we really need a lantern," Kayo added.

"You were in my house," the man said. "Saw you come out."

Kayo removed her Texas Rangers baseball cap, smoothed back her hair, and replaced the cap.

"Well, yes, we did go in," Rosie said. "We knocked first, and when there wasn't any answer, we went in to see if we could find help, to get us back home."

"You saw my birds."

"Yes," Kayo said. "They're—the birds are beautiful. It must take you a long time to do each one."

The man nodded. "Not easy to skin a bird," he said. "Have to clean all the flesh and fat off the feathers."

Rosie swallowed hard. I don't want to hear

this, she thought. I don't want to know how it's done.

"You're a real expert," Kayo said.

Rosie knew what Kayo was doing. She was trying to compliment the man so that he would have good feelings toward Rosie and Kayo. If he had good feelings, he might step aside and let them leave.

"Have to put cotton in the eye sockets," the man said.

Rosie closed her eyes, feeling faint. She was already tired and hungry and scared. Thinking about how a taxidermist does his work was more than her stomach could take. She reached out and rested one hand on the arm of the rocking chair.

"It's been real nice talking to you," Kayo said, "but we have to go now."

Rosie's eyes flew open. Something in Kayo's voice alerted her. She's going to run for it, Rosie thought. If he tries to make us stay here, Kayo's going to take a chance and try to jump past him and run off into the forest.

The man shook his head slowly from side to side. "Can't leave," he said.

He put both hands out sideways, completely blocking the steps. The lantern swung back and forth from one outstretched hand, making a moving shadow on the porch.

47

Flattery didn't work, Rosie thought. Maybe I can scare him into letting us go.

"If we stay here," Rosie said, "a search party will come looking for us. By now, my parents have notified the sheriff and the highway patrol and all kinds of people. They'll all come into the woods looking for us, and, sooner or later, someone will find your cabin, and then all those people will come tramping in, and they'll be followed by television news people, and they'll all see your birds, too, and they'll ask you where you got them."

"That's right," Kayo said. "If you don't want a whole lot of people here, you'd better let us leave right now."

The man's face contorted in anger. "No people!" he shouted. He lunged forward and grabbed Kayo's arm.

"Run!" Kayo shouted.

Rosie leaped off the porch and dashed past the man. She ran down the short path past the rock with the squirrel skin.

Behind her, Kayo twisted and pulled, trying to free herself from the man's grasp.

He still held the lantern in one hand, and Kayo took advantage of that by leaning toward the light. The man was strong, but Kayo was strong, too.

Rosie stopped, out of the circle of light, and watched.

The man bent forward, still holding on to Kayo, and set the lantern on the porch. Then he grabbed Kayo with both hands.

Rosie looked around for a large branch to use as a weapon.

"Help!" Kayo cried.

It was too dark to find a branch, Rosie thought, and she wasn't sure she was strong enough to knock the man out even if she did find one.

Rosie faced away from the cabin, looking into the dark, empty woods beside her. "Here we are!" she shouted. "Over this way! Hurry!" Then she turned and yelled back toward the cabin. "Kayo! They've found us! Here comes the search party!"

The man and Kayo stopped wrestling and turned toward Rosie. For one brief second, while the man looked for the reported search party, he loosened his hold. Instantly, Kayo wrenched herself free and took off.

As soon as Kayo was out of the man's grip, Rosie turned and ran away. She knew Kayo would catch up to her; Kayo was a much faster runner than Rosie was.

The man stared after Kayo for a moment before he realized that Rosie had tricked him. There was no rescue party. There were no people coming through the woods.

He grabbed the lantern and started after the girls. Anger made a muscle in the side of his neck twitch. He would catch those two kids. No sweat.

They were lost, but he knew every tree and bush in these woods for miles in all directions. He could draw a map of this forest with his eyes closed.

There was no way two lost kids could escape from him.

Not here. Not at night.

Chapter

7

It was too dark to run fast.

The girls pushed through the undergrowth, not caring if their faces got scratched. Kayo quickly caught up to Rosie and took the lead. She moved with her hands outstretched in front of her, to make sure she didn't crash into a tree, lifting her feet high so she wouldn't trip.

"He's a madman," Rosie said. Her words came in short puffs.

"Why would he want to keep us there?" Kayo said. "You'd think he would be glad to get rid of us."

Rosie looked back over her shoulder. In the distance, she saw the lantern light. "He's following us," Rosie said.

"Maybe he will only chase us a short way, to make sure we really leave. Maybe he'll turn back soon."

"He was so angry!" Rosie said. "He acted as if we had tried to steal his birds, when all we did was look at them."

"He knows it's against the law to kill those birds," Kayo said. "He's afraid we'll tell."

"He's right," Rosie puffed. "We *will* tell, and when we do . . . oh!" Rosie tripped on a tree root that bulged underfoot and lost her balance. She grabbed for the tree trunk, to steady herself, but her hand grazed across the rough bark, and she tumbled to the ground.

"Kayo!" Rosie cried. "Wait! I fell."

Kayo turned back to where Rosie lay on the ground. "Are you okay?" she said, extending a hand to help Rosie get up.

Rosie got to her feet and limped a few steps forward. "I turned my ankle," she said. "I didn't break anything, but I can't keep going."

"You have to," Kayo said, glancing nervously back at the lantern.

The man was half a city block behind them, but the light from his lantern reached high into the treetops, creating a bright patch of fear. "He's gaining on us," Kayo said.

"You go on without me," Rosie said. "I'll never be able to outrun him now."

"I can't leave you," Kayo said.

"There's no sense in both of us getting

caught," Rosie said. "When you find the road, send someone back to help me."

"What if I don't find the road? We were lost before we found the cabin, and we're just as lost now. I might not find my way out."

"You have to," Rosie said. "It's our only chance."

The girls stood close together, barely able to see each other in the darkness.

"Maybe you can hide from him," Kayo said. "Lie down, and I'll cover you with leaves."

Rosie dropped to her knees and then stretched out next to a large tree that had been felled by a storm. She lay as close to the tree as she could, wedging one arm underneath it.

The light grew brighter.

"Hurry," Rosie said, "or he'll catch us."

Kayo bent and gathered leaves and twigs from the forest floor. She threw them on top of Rosie, covering Rosie's legs. She threw more leaves on Rosie's body, until only Rosie's head stuck out. "I'll hide as much of your face as I can," she said, "without smothering you."

Kayo scooped up more leaves and carefully piled them on Rosie's cheeks and forehead. "If he sees your nose," she said, "maybe he'll think it's a mushroom."

Light flickered on the tree trunks.

"He's close," Rosie said.

Kayo placed two brown leaves on the lenses of Rosie's glasses. "Good luck," she whispered. "Don't move."

"Run!" Rosie said, without moving her lips.

Kayo sprinted away from the approaching lantern light, fleeing alone into the dark forest.

Rosie lay still, listening to Kayo's footsteps disappear. Her dread of the man and her anxiety over being lost were pushed aside by an even deeper emotion.

What if I never see Kayo again? Rosie thought. What if my best friend disappears into the forest and is never found?

Rosie had never felt so alone, or so afraid.

Seconds after Kayo's footsteps ran away, other, heavier footsteps approached. Rosie listened to the crunch of leaves and snapping of twigs as the big man stomped toward her.

What if he steps on me? she thought. What if he comes toward this fallen tree and puts his foot smack on my face? What if these leaves make me sneeze?

As soon as she thought about sneezing, her nose tickled. She wriggled her nose and inhaled through her mouth until the tickle subsided.

Thump. Thump. Thump. The footsteps came closer.

Rosie lay still as a stick, barely breathing, trying to tell how close the man was. Her heart pounded so hard she was sure he would hear it.

The earthy scent of rotting leaves mixed with dirt filled her nose. It smelled like her dad's compost pile.

She felt another tickle, on her neck this time. But this tickle, Rosie realized, wasn't just an imagined itch. Something was crawling on her skin.

Some live thing had crawled onto her bare neck and was now creeping around the leaves, up the side of her face. Rosie pressed her lips together and tried to stay calm.

Maybe it's only an ant, Rosie told herself. I can stand to lie here and let an ant crawl across me. But what if it's something worse than an ant? What if it's a spider? She shuddered slightly. Spiders were not high on Rosie's list of favorite creatures.

What if it's a snake? Or a slimy slug?

It took every bit of willpower she possessed to keep her hands quietly at her sides while the slug/ant/spider/snake crept past the corner of her eye and crawled toward her forehead.

She kept expecting it to bite her. What if it was poisonous? Tears oozed from the corners of Rosie's eyes, trickled past her cheekbones, and puddled in her ears.

After a minute or so, she didn't feel the crawling anymore. Had whatever it was crawled back onto the ground? Or was it in her hair, crawling along on top of her head, where it could easily return to her face?

Crunch. A foot landed just inches from Rosie's knee. Rosie's breathing became fast and shallow. In her concern over what was crawling on her face, she had not realized the man was so close.

She couldn't see him, of course, with the leaves on her glasses, but she knew he was there.

A small twig snapped as his other foot landed beside her shoulder. If she wanted to, she could reach out and grab the man's ankles.

Don't look down, she thought. *Please, please, don't look down.*

Her stomach rumbled. To Rosie, it sounded identical to the growling sound Bone Breath made whenever Webster walked too close to Bone Breath's bowl during doggie dinner. Rosie was sure the man would hear the noise and discover her hiding place.

She clenched her teeth and held her breath, expecting two large hands to grab her and yank her to her feet.

"I see you!" he bellowed.

Rosie twitched as the sudden loud voice exploded above her.

"I see you," he yelled again. "You can't get away!"

The log beside her sank slightly as the man placed one foot on top of it. He stepped down on the other side.

The footsteps moved on, thudding away from the log where Rosie lay and going in the direction Kayo had run.

He was yelling at Kayo, Rosie realized. He didn't hear my stomach growl; he didn't see me at all. He can probably hear Kayo in the woods ahead of him, and maybe, with the lantern, he can see her, too. But he didn't see me. He still thinks Kayo and I are together, so he never looked down. He never knew I was right there next to him.

Rosie lay quietly, giving her pounding heart a chance to settle down. As her tense muscles relaxed a bit, she debated what to do. Should she stay there on the ground, hidden by the leaves, and wait for help to arrive? Or should she get to her feet and limp in the opposite direction from where Kayo and the man were headed?

What if the man decided he couldn't catch Kayo? Kayo was strong and fast. What if the man gave up soon and came back this way? If he spotted Rosie, she would never get away from him again. She wasn't that fast to begin with, and now, with her ankle throbbing, she could barely walk.

I'm too tired to start walking again, Rosie decided. My ankle hurts, and I need to rest awhile. If I force myself to keep moving now, I'll end up so exhausted I'll probably collapse.

It was not too uncomfortable, lying there beside the fallen tree. Although the ground was hard, the tree trunk beside her and the leaves Kayo had heaped on top of her provided protection from the mosquitoes.

She raised one hand and brushed the leaves off her glasses.

She opened her eyes and stared straight up through the branches of the trees. High above her, a single star shone brightly in the black sky. Somehow, the sight was comforting.

If Mom and Dad look at the sky right now, Rosie thought, they will see the same star I see. It's visible from my backyard at home, and from the patio behind Kayo's apartment. My cousins in Indiana can walk outside and see that very star, shining in the night sky.

Star light, star bright. First star I've seen tonight. I wish I may, I wish I might, have the wish I wish tonight.

The old rhyme ran through Rosie's mind. She liked to believe it was true. At home, she always squeezed her eyes tight at the first glimpse of a star, and made a wish.

Now, as she lay alone in the woods listening for the scary man to return, she kept her eyes open. But she still made a fervent wish.

I wish, Rosie thought, *I wish that Kayo and I would get home safely.*

Chapter

8

Kayo heard the man's shout behind her. For an instant, she thought he had discovered Rosie.

The lantern light moved closer. He didn't see Rosie, Kayo realized. He sees me. Those few seconds spent scooping up leaves to hide Rosie had cost Kayo most of her lead. She wondered what else they would cost her.

She did not need to look behind her to see the light now. Dim rays danced ahead of her, causing shadows in the trees. The glow pursued her, threatening to overtake her. Kayo felt surrounded by danger.

Kayo tried to think what she should do. She couldn't elude him much longer. She was too tired, and the man was too close. Eventually, he would catch her.

What then? Would he drag her back to the

cabin? Why? She could think of no reason for the man's odd behavior other than the opinion Rosie had voiced. "He's a madman," Rosie had said, and Kayo thought Rosie was right.

She had no idea in which direction she was moving. Was she going toward help or deeper into the forest?

She considered trying to hide from the man. She could find a sturdy tree and climb it and hope the man did not see her. But what if he did? If the man saw her climb a tree, there would be no way down except to drop to the dirt beside him. That plan might have worked when she was far ahead of him, but it would not work when he was so close.

The binoculars thumped against Kayo's chest as she ran. She yanked the strap over her head and carried it. The binoculars could be a weapon, she thought. I could swing the strap and smack the man with the heavy binoculars.

She had no desire to hit the man with any-thing, and she would avoid it if possible. He was bigger and stronger than she was, and she did not want to fight with him. She hoped he would not catch her, but if he did, and if she had no choice but to defend herself, it was comforting to know she had something to use besides her bare hands.

Kayo's breath came in short gasps now. Her physical training for baseball had not prepared her for this. She could run laps around the smooth track at school; she could sprint around the bases from home plate to first, to second. But she was not used to thick undergrowth, to spongy leaves that sank beneath her weight, or to tree branches that snagged her sweatshirt and slowed her progress.

She felt like a hamster in an exercise wheel—running and running but getting nowhere.

Should she stop and confront him? He had been willing enough to talk earlier about his success with the divining rod and his skills as a taxidermist. Maybe, Kayo thought, I should give up and go back to the cabin with him and try to keep him talking while I wait for someone to find me.

She knew Mr. and Mrs. Saunders would have reported the girls missing by now. A search was already under way; Kayo was certain of that. With any luck, the searchers would find the two bicycles. When they did, they surely would climb the gravel road and spread out from there.

Search-and-rescue teams are accustomed to rough terrain; they would move quickly. Maybe they'll bring a search dog, Kayo thought. A bloodhound or a German shepherd would find us in a hurry. Maybe Rosie's parents are even using Bone Breath.

Whatever method the searchers used, Kayo

hoped they would find her soon. Too bad I can't blow the whistle, she thought. The whistle might help the searchers find her—but if there were no searchers nearby, it would only help the man who had stolen the eagle to keep track of her.

Even with the hope of help arriving, Kayo was reluctant to let the man near her. His earlier anger, his furious shouts in the woods, and his theft of the baby eagle all indicated he was not a normal person.

Everything about the man was weird. He was a crazy hermit who lived in the forest, and there was no way to tell what he would do. Kayo kept running.

The dense undergrowth ended; trees were suddenly sparse. Ahead of her, moonlight shone on a flat meadow. Kayo's legs went into high speed. She flew across the clearing, easily pulling ahead of the man again.

On the far side of the meadow, the top of an old cedar tree pointed toward the ground. The tree was broken in half about ten feet up, as if it had been struck by lightning. Instead of running past the tree, Kayo hoisted herself onto the broken trunk and scrambled up it.

Jagged edges of bark stuck into the air where the tree had splintered. The center of the stump was hollow partway down. Kayo snapped a limb off the tree trunk and then climbed into the stump, curving herself into a tight ball. She placed the broken limb on her shoulders, with the tip covering her head. She could see over the edge of the stump, and if the man looked up, he would see her.

The light grew brighter as it crossed the meadow. He came closer. Closer. He stopped at the edge of the forest, six feet from the hollow cedar, and looked around, as if unsure which way to go.

Kayo waited.

He held the lantern to his right and then to his left, looking and listening. But he never looked up. After a few moments, he walked back into the meadow, turned right, and moved away.

Kayo watched the lantern light grow dimmer. At the far end of the meadow, it disappeared into the forest. Kayo unfolded her cramped body and climbed out of the tree stump. When her feet touched the ground, she realized her legs were shaking.

Kayo wondered what Rosie was doing. Was she still lying next to the log, hiding? Or had she hobbled off in the other direction as soon as the man passed her?

I don't like being separated, Kayo thought. Even when we're in trouble, I'd rather be together.

Across the meadow, far to her right, a faint

glow flashed between the trees. In a few seconds, there was another glimmer of light. The gleam of the lantern was moving away from her, growing fainter by the second. He must be going home.

Kayo decided to follow him. Even though she was afraid of the man, and worried about what he might do if he caught her, she feared being all alone in the forest even more. She would follow the man, keeping far enough back that he didn't know she was there.

She was sure he would return to his cabin. Kayo decided she would go there, too. Although the man claimed he never got supplies, she didn't see how he could live in complete isolation, having no contact with the rest of the world. He would need matches and flour. What about the cotton he had said he used? He must go to town once in a while, Kayo thought, or someone brings him what he needs.

Either way, there would be some kind of path or trail leading out of the woods from the cabin to the road. Kayo decided she would hide near the cabin until the man went to sleep. Then she would search for that path and follow it.

Stepping softly through the darkness, Kayo headed across the clearing toward the trees where she had glimpsed the lantern light.

*   *   *

After Rosie wished on the star, she lay quietly for several minutes. Her ankle felt better.

She thought about her wish to get safely home. I won't get there by lying here under a pile of leaves, Rosie thought. I need to get up, and—and what? Go where? Her thoughts whirled like a windmill in a storm.

She sat up, brushing the leaves from her arms, and looked around. The moon had come up. Faint moonlight seeped between the treetops, making the dark shapes of trees and bushes more visible.

I should try to find my way back to the cabin, she decided. While the man chases Kayo, I need to go back and look for another lantern. With light, perhaps I can find the stones that Kayo put in the trees. I can retrace our steps. Maybe I can find my way back to the gravel road.

A light would be visible to anyone looking for us. It might even shine up through the treetops and be spotted by someone in a search helicopter.

She got to her feet, gingerly putting weight on the sore ankle. It still hurt, but it did not throb the way it had at first. The sprain isn't as bad as I thought, Rosie decided. I can still walk on it.

She slid the toe of her shoe across the ground, feeling for the root that had tripped her. When she found it, she knew which way she had been running when she fell.

Rosie inhaled deeply and headed back the way

she had come. Think positive, she told herself. I'll find the cabin. I'll go in and find a lantern or other source of light. I'll get a drink of water. With any luck, I'll find some bread or fruit.

She swatted at her face. Maybe, she thought, I'll find some mosquito repellent.

She moved slowly, squinting in the dim moonlight. She looked for broken branches or other indications that she was retracing her earlier steps.

About once a minute, she stood still and listened.

She hoped she would hear rescuers shouting her name; she feared she would hear the strange man's footsteps behind her.

Chapter

*T*hey should be back by now." Mr. Saunders looked at his watch for the tenth time. "Maybe one of the bikes had a flat tire."

"They may have had an accident," Mrs. Saunders said. "I think we should drive on and look for them."

Mr. Saunders agreed. "They rode east," he said. "If we go that way, too, there's no way we could miss them if they're headed back here."

He grasped the metal fold-down step that made it easier to step from the motor home to the ground, and slid it up under the door. Mrs. Saunders fastened the sliding bathroom door so it wouldn't bang open while they drove.

They both put their coffee cups in the sink, so the cups wouldn't fall off the table and break.

When everything was secure, Mr. Saunders

started the engine. He drove slowly, letting his eyes roam along the edges of the road. Mrs. Saunders sat on the other side of the motor home, staring at the shoulder of the road on her side.

Bone Breath, seeming to sense that something was wrong, jumped on the sofa, stood on his hind legs, and pressed his nose to the window, too.

They saw no sign of the girls or their bicycles.

Mr. Saunders turned around at the small town of Newhalem. "They would not have ridden this far," he said.

They drove back toward the spot where they had parked earlier.

"If they had an accident," Mrs. Saunders said, "a motorist might have stopped to help. Someone may have driven them to a doctor."

Mr. Saunders nodded grimly and kept driving. He thought if a motorist had stopped to help two children who had a bicycle accident, that motorist surely would have sent word somehow to the parents of those children. But he didn't say so. His wife was worried enough without having him suggest that someone picked up the girls but did not take them to get help.

"The sun is going down," Mrs. Saunders said.

Mr. Saunders pulled into the picnic area where they had parked earlier. Mrs. Saunders reached for their cellular phone and called 911.

Minutes later, a green car with a gold star on

the side arrived at the phone booth. On the star were the words "Skagit County Sheriff."

"I spoke with the highway patrol," the sheriff said. "There was no report of any accident on Highway 20 today."

A check with the nearest hospital revealed no twelve-year-old girls had been admitted or treated.

"I'd like you to wait here," the sheriff said. "I've called in a search-and-rescue team, and they can use the motor home as a base."

"Do you use dogs?" Mr. Saunders asked.

"We would if the girls had been on foot," the sheriff replied, "but the search dogs can't follow bicycle tires."

"How long will it take the searchers to get here?" Mrs. Saunders asked.

"An hour. Maybe two."

"Could we continue to drive along the road, too, for a while longer?" Mrs. Saunders asked. "We'll go crazy if we just sit in the motor home and wait."

"Go ahead," the sheriff said. "We'll meet here in forty-five minutes."

Mr. and Mrs. Saunders drove east again, hoping for some clue. Bone Breath stared out the window.

"We couldn't see anything in daylight," Mrs.

Saunders said as they cruised slowly down the road. "It's worse now that it's getting dark."

Bone Breath barked.

Mr. Saunders put his foot on the brake. Mrs. Saunders got out of her seat and went to look out the window beside Bone Breath.

"I don't see anything," she said. "We just passed that gravel road again. I wonder if Bone Breath saw something there."

Mr. Saunders pulled the motor home as far onto the shoulder of the road as he could. "There isn't room to park," he said.

"You stay here, in case you have to move, and I'll go look where Bone Breath barked," Mrs. Saunders said. "He probably saw a deer or a raccoon, but at this point we have to be sure."

"Why don't you take Bone Breath with you?" Mr. Saunders suggested. "Maybe he barked because he needs a walk."

Mrs. Saunders put Bone Breath's harness on him and snapped the leash to the harness. She jumped to the ground without bothering with the fold-down step, and Bone Breath followed. She walked around the back of the motor home, looked both ways for traffic, and led Bone Breath toward the gravel road.

Bone Breath trotted eagerly beside her.

"You're glad for the exercise, aren't you?" Mrs.

Saunders said. Then she added, "Where's Rosie? Can you find Rosie?"

Bone Breath wagged his tail and tugged forward.

When they reached the gravel road, Mrs. Saunders stopped. She looked around, but it was nearly dark out now, and she saw nothing to indicate that Rosie and Kayo had been there.

She turned and started back to the motor home. Instead of trotting out in front of her as he had before, Bone Breath lagged behind, sniffing the ground.

Mrs. Saunders tugged on the leash. "Come on, Bone Breath," she said. "Let's go."

Bone Breath whined and kept sniffing.

Mrs. Saunders stepped to where the cairn terrier stood. "What do you smell?" she asked. "Do you smell Rosie?"

Bone Breath barked, one short, sharp bark.

Mrs. Saunders felt a mixture of hope and foolishness. Chances are, she thought, Bone Breath smells a rabbit or a coyote. She looked down the road and saw her husband standing outside the motor home, watching her.

"Bring the flashlight!" she yelled. "Bone Breath smells something."

Mr. Saunders turned the motor home's warning flashers on. The red lights blinked on and off, on and off, as he grabbed the flashlight and dashed toward his wife.

"Bone Breath keeps sniffing this road," Mrs. Saunders explained. "It may be wishful thinking that he smells Rosie, but I wonder if the girls turned here and went up the hill."

Shining the flashlight back and forth on the ground, Mr. Saunders strode up the gravel road, with Mrs. Saunders and Bone Breath beside him.

They climbed for several minutes but saw nothing unusual.

"It's time for us to meet the sheriff," Mrs. Saunders said. "Let's tell him about this road and how Bone Breath acted. The rescue crews are better equipped to search than we are."

Mr. and Mrs. Saunders turned and started back down the road. Bone Breath whined and pulled in the other direction.

"Come!" Mrs. Saunders said, giving the leash a yank.

Bone Breath braced his legs and refused to budge.

Mrs. Saunders went back, keeping the leash taut so Bone Breath couldn't walk farther up the hill. She picked him up and carried him down the road.

As they walked, Mr. Saunders continued to wave the flashlight from one side of the road to the other.

When they were almost back to where the gravel road joined the highway, he aimed the flashlight at a clump of bushes. Metal glinted in the light. Probably a discarded pop can, he thought, but he went closer and shined his light behind the bushes.

"I found the bikes!" he yelled.

"Yip!" cried Bone Breath. He struggled out of Mrs. Saunders's arms and jumped to the ground.

"Rosie!" Mr. Saunders called. "Kayo! Can you hear me?"

Quickly, he flashed the light all around the bushes, looking for any other sign of the two girls.

"Let's leave the bikes here," Mrs. Saunders suggested. "The police will want to see exactly where they are. It may help them decide if the girls hid the bikes themselves, or if someone else dumped them. And they may want to check for fingerprints."

The only way they could get Bone Breath to leave the bicycles was to carry him again. Mrs. Saunders gathered the little dog in her arms and ran back to the motor home.

As soon as she got in the motor home, Mrs. Saunders read the mileage so she could tell the police exactly how far it was to the bicycles.

Mr. Saunders drove quickly toward the picnic

area where they had agreed to meet. A highway patrol car was already there.

Mrs. Saunders looked at the mileage again and then jumped out and told the two officers what they had found and where. Seconds later, blue lights whirled in the dark night as the patrol car headed toward the gravel road. The officers broadcast a general call instructing the search-and-rescue squad and other officers to meet there, too, as soon as possible.

Chapter

10

Kayo stalked the man. Stealthily, she crept behind the arc of lantern light, following it through the woods.

As long as she stayed close, she could see well enough to avoid bumping into trees or crashing unexpectedly through low brush.

It helped that the man was walking now, instead of running. It was easier for Kayo to move quietly when she could take her time.

The man seemed to know where he was. He never stopped to look around, as if getting his bearings, and he never changed his direction. He just kept going, holding up the lantern to light his way.

While Kayo tailed the man and spied on him, Rosie hobbled through the forest. The towering trees blocked out most of the moonlight, making it too dark to run, even if she had been able to. She groped in front of her, as a blind person would, feeling her way.

Her bones ached. Her muscles ached. Her ankle ached. If it's possible to have aching hair, Rosie thought, I have it.

She longed to soak in a hot bath, with her eyes closed and her head resting on the back of the tub.

Instead, she forced her tired legs to keep moving. She was afraid if she stopped walking, her muscles would stiffen up and she wouldn't be able to run if she needed to. She swatted her neck again and imagined being eaten by giant mosquitoes.

Right foot, left foot, right foot. Rosie stumbled wearily on.

As Rosie walked, she thought about the hermit who lived in the cabin. She wondered why anyone would cut himself off from the rest of the world. What was his background? Was he hiding from the police? If so, what had he done?

It could be anything, Rosie thought. Maybe he refuses to pay income taxes. Maybe he stole money from his employer and got caught so he ran away.

Maybe he's a murderer.

That last idea seemed entirely plausible to

Rosie. Even if the man had not murdered a person, he seemed to have no qualms about murdering healthy, beautiful birds. She wondered what he had done with the eaglet.

She shuddered. Don't think about him, she told herself. Think about something good. Think about being back with Mom and Dad and Bone Breath, safe in the motor home. Think about returning home Sunday night, and Webster will rub on my ankles and purr when he sees me. Think about school on Monday morning, and how Kayo and I will have an adventure to tell about, and it will make Sammy Hulenback jealous because our lives are exciting and his isn't.

Rosie sighed. Right now, she thought, I'd trade my excitement in a minute for Sammy's dull, safe life.

After trailing the man for a long time, Kayo saw a little wooden structure ahead. It was only four feet square, much smaller than the log cabin, and it had no windows.

The man walked straight to the tiny building, yanked open the door, and went inside.

Immediately, Kayo realized what it was. An outhouse. She had never actually seen an outhouse before, but she had read about them in books.

This is probably where the man was earlier,

when we first found the cabin, Kayo thought. While we were calling and knocking on his door, he was out here, using the outhouse.

If that was so, the cabin must be close by. No one would want to walk any farther than necessary, especially in the winter. Kayo peered into the woods, but, even with the help of the moon, she could see only a foot ahead without the lantern light.

While she waited for the man to come out, she considered using the outhouse herself. The power of suggestion, Kayo thought. I didn't have to go until I started thinking about it.

Rosie nearly missed the log cabin. Lost in her thoughts, she walked almost all the way past the back side of it without looking in that direction. At the last moment, the far corner caught her eye.

Rosie's aches were chased away by her racing blood as she tiptoed around the cabin to the front. No light came through the window; the man must not have returned.

Rosie gazed all around at the forest. She saw no lantern glow. She heard no footsteps.

Here's my chance, she thought. I'll go in and look for a lantern and some food. Maybe she would even take one of the stuffed eagles or the spotted owl, as evidence for the police that the man killed birds illegally.

As she climbed the porch steps, it occurred to her that the man may have returned and gone to bed. What if he was asleep just inside the cabin door?

The only way to find out was to go in.

When she started to lift the wooden door latch, it made a creaking sound. Rosie stopped. She did not intend to announce her presence by making a racket as she entered. She tried pushing the latch against the door as she lifted; it creaked again.

Rosie hunched over the latch, wiggled it gently back and forth, and then pulled it toward her while she raised it. This time, the latch lifted smoothly, with only a tiny squeak.

Rosie glanced behind her one more time before she pushed the door open.

Kayo saw the outhouse door open. The man stepped out, letting the door bang shut behind him. Both arms hung at his sides now, so the lantern lit only a small area around his feet.

Kayo watched, making sure she saw which way he went. When he was well ahead of her, she moved toward the outhouse.

Just before she reached the door, she looked

down. A path led away from the outhouse; the man had taken the path.

Kayo knew she would be able to find the cabin now, even if she lost sight of the man. All she had to do was follow the path.

She opened the outhouse door, glad that it didn't creak, and slipped inside. A terrible stench greeted her.

Yuck! Kayo thought. She raised one shoulder and buried her nose in her sweatshirt, trying not to inhale the odor. She wondered if the man who didn't believe in telephones or cars might believe in toilet paper. Apparently not, she decided.

She finished quickly, stepped outside, and took a deep gulp of fresh air. Keeping her eyes down, she slipped along the path after the man.

Soon she saw the lantern ahead and, beyond it, the dark outline of the cabin.

I'm here, Kayo thought. I made it without him hearing me. All I have to do now is wait until he goes inside and falls asleep. Then I'll hunt for whatever trail connects the cabin with the rest of the world.

Kayo stopped where she could see the cabin through the brush. Wearily, she leaned against a tree. I'll rest, she decided, until I'm sure he's asleep. I'll wait for a half hour after no light shines from his window; then I'll search for a path.

She watched as the man approached the cabin.

He walked to the steps, picked up the tin bucket that lay on the bottom step, and carried it away from the cabin. The lantern light disappeared behind a clump of trees.

In order to see what he was doing, Kayo had to move through the woods to her right.

The man put the lantern on the ground and positioned the bucket under the spout of a small pump.

Kayo hid behind a tree and watched.

With the lantern on the ground beside him, the man's face was lit from below. He grasped the pump handle and worked it up and down. Shadows rippled like waves across the trees behind him as the man moved his arms.

Water gushed from the pump opening into the bucket. The man lifted the bucket and drank from it. Next, he dipped both hands into the water and splashed it on his face. He shook his head the way a dog shakes to remove water, and wiped his hands on his pants.

When he finished washing, the man carried the bucket to a cleared patch of ground and emptied the rest of the water at the base of a group of small branches arranged in a tepee shape.

Kayo was too far away to be certain, but she thought the man was watering pea plants or pole beans or some other climbing vegetable that needs support.

He returned to the pump, filled the bucket with fresh water, and, with the bucket in one hand and the lantern in the other, walked back toward the front of the cabin.

When he came out from behind the trees and saw the front of the cabin, he stopped.

"Hey!" he yelled.

Kayo nearly jumped out of her shoes at the sudden shout.

The man ran toward the porch steps. "I see you!" he hollered as he ran.

Kayo tried to see who the man was shouting at. Had rescuers arrived? Were Rosie's parents here? Kayo breathed faster, thinking of the possibilities.

The man stopped at the bottom of the steps and set the bucket of water on the ground. He straightened up, holding the lantern shoulder high.

Kayo moved quietly to her left and looked past the man, straining to see who was there.

Her mouth dropped open. It was not a rescue team. It was not Mr. and Mrs. Saunders.

A lone figure stood on the porch, with her back to the latched door. She held a slice of bread in one hand and a stuffed eagle in the other.

Kayo stared in dismay as the lantern light flickered across Rosie's frightened face.

83

Chapter

11

The man lunged up the steps toward Rosie.

"Stop!" screamed Kayo. "Don't hurt her!"

The man whirled around and looked behind him. Kayo stayed hidden behind the trees.

Rosie dropped the bread and the eagle as she bolted to her left. She ran to the end of the porch, ducked under the porch railing, and jumped to the ground.

The man clomped across the porch after her. He grabbed for Rosie just as she went under the railing. He caught the bottom of her jacket and jerked on it, but he could not hold on. The fabric slipped from his fingers as Rosie's feet hit the ground.

"This way!" Kayo yelled. "Run, Rosie! Run!"

Rosie dashed across the clearing toward Kayo's voice.

The man ran back to the steps, stomped down them, and headed toward Rosie. With his eyes fastened on her, he did not notice the bucket of water on the ground.

His foot landed on the edge of the bucket, tipping the bucket toward him. Water splashed across his shoes as the man lost his balance. His arms flailed the air; when he tried to step sideways, to catch his balance, the bucket stayed on his foot.

The man fell forward. His head made a dull *thud* as it hit the large rock where the squirrel skin was spread to dry.

The lantern flew out of his hand and hit the rock, too. Shattered pieces of glass hopped across the ground like flat stones skipped on the surface of a lake. The lantern bounced into the air and landed on its side in a patch of weeds on the other side of the rock.

"Hurry!" Kayo shouted.

The man lay sprawled on the ground.

Rosie raced toward Kayo.

Kerosene leaked out of the broken lantern. The lantern flame burned brighter and then spread in a widening circle. Weeds ignited. Fallen twigs burst into flame.

The man lay where he had fallen.

Kayo ran out of the trees toward the cabin to

meet Rosie. The girls looked at the motionless man.

"Do you think he's dead?" Rosie whispered.

"I'm not touching him to find out," Kayo replied.

The fire expanded. Fingers of flame crawled toward the corner of the cabin. Sparks leaped into the air as a twig crackled and split in half. A separate, small fire ignited closer to the edge of the woods.

"The cabin is going to burn," Rosie said, "and the man with it."

"The whole forest could go up in smoke," Kayo said.

"All the trees," Rosie said. "The deer. The bear. The eagle nests."

"And us," Kayo said.

The girls looked at each other for a fraction of a second longer, but they both knew what they had to do. Without saying a word, they went into action.

Kayo ran past the inert body of the man, grabbed the bucket, and dashed around the clump of trees toward the pump.

While Kayo rushed to the pump, Rosie raced toward the circle of fire. She stomped on the smallest flames, moving her feet fast. She took off her jacket and beat at the fire, smothering it so it could not spread toward the forest.

Kayo put the bucket under the pump and jerked the handle up and down as fast as she could. When the bucket was full, she raced back and dumped the water on the flames closest to the cabin. The fire sputtered and smoked.

Kayo didn't wait to see if it went completely out or not. She rushed back to the pump and filled the bucket again.

Rosie slapped her jacket on a burning twig.

The man groaned and rubbed his head but did not open his eyes.

"He's alive," Rosie said when Kayo returned. She wasn't sure if that was good news or not.

Glowing sparks jumped in all directions. Red, yellow, and blue flames sprouted from the surface of the earth where the sparks landed. The patches of fire were small—a few leaves here, a bit of weed there—but each was potentially disastrous.

The fire is spreading faster than I can put it out, Rosie thought. I need more than this light jacket.

She ran up the porch steps and yanked on the latch, no longer caring how much noise she made.

Kayo returned with another bucket of water. Thinking that she would stop the fire at its source, she ran through the scattering of low flames to the broken lantern and poured the water on top of it.

Instantly, the ring of fire got wider. Instead of putting the fire out, the water on the burning kerosene helped the flames spread. The kerosene floated on the water, moving outward in all directions from the smashed lantern. Clumps of weeds and grass flared quickly, illuminating the clearing.

Kayo backed away from the fire. She remembered when her mother had once answered the phone as she heated cooking oil in a pan. While Mrs. Benton talked, the oil overheated and burst into flame. Instead of throwing the pan into the sink and running water on it, Mrs. Benton had snatched an open box of baking soda and dumped the contents onto the hot oil.

"Oil and water don't mix," she had told Kayo as they scrubbed smoke from the back of the stove. "Never put water on a grease fire or burning oil. Such fires have to be smothered."

As Kayo ran back to the pump for more water, she mentally kicked herself for not remembering her mother's warning. Water was great for drenching the leaves and grass and twigs that caught fire, but it would not work on the spilled kerosene.

While Kayo pumped the pail full again, Rosie

pushed the door open and entered the cabin. She immediately turned left, where she knew the bed was. She yanked a heavy wool blanket from the bed and rushed back outside with it.

Holding one side of the blanket, she threw it down as hard as she could on the flames. Then, leaving the blanket on the ground, she stamped her feet on top of the blanket.

I hope the blanket doesn't catch fire, she thought. If it does, the flames are likely to leap up my jeans before I can get away.

She smelled scorched wool. She jumped off the blanket, tugged at the edge, and pulled it away from the fire. Smoke curled upward where the blanket had been, but she saw no flames on the ground in that spot.

Rosie picked up the smoldering blanket and threw it on the lantern. The smell of burning wool intensified. Dark smoke rose from a spot in the center of the blanket.

Kayo returned with another bucket of water.

"Throw the water on the blanket this time," Rosie said. "I'm afraid it's going to catch fire."

Kayo tossed the contents of the bucket across the center of the blanket. "It will work better if it's damp," she said.

The blanket sizzled and hissed, sending spirals of steam into the air.

Kayo poured the next bucketful all around the edges of the blanket.

The water made the blanket heavier. Rosie's arms ached as she struggled to lift it and throw it down again. Now I know why someone who stifles the fun is called a wet blanket, she thought.

Kayo sloshed water across the bottom step of the cabin.

"Good thinking," Rosie said. "If the step is wet, it won't catch."

Kayo didn't stop to answer; she dashed back to the pump.

Rosie raised the damp blanket shoulder high and dropped it on a small shrub that had burst into flame. She kicked the bottom of the blanket in around the base of the shrub, trying to seal off the oxygen.

"Arrgggh!" An animal-like sound ripped through the night. Terrified, Rosie turned toward the sound and realized it had come from the still-unconscious man. The man's shirt sleeve was on fire.

"Kayo!" Rosie screamed.

Kayo dashed around the corner with a half-full bucket of water.

Rosie jerked the blanket off the bush and ran to the man. Kayo dumped the water on his burning sleeve. Rosie threw the blanket across the man,

90

covering all but his head. She dropped to her knees beside him and pressed the blanket against his arm for a moment.

The man groaned.

Rosie stood up and pulled the blanket off. The fire on his arm was out.

"We have to move him away from the fire," Kayo said.

"Hurry." Rosie flung the blanket down on the flames nearest her and left it there. She leaned over the man and pushed on his shoulders.

Kayo shoved on his hips. Slowly, they rolled the man away from the cabin, toward the forest. It was hard to push a heavy person along the uneven ground. Rosie's back hurt from bending down. Kayo dug in her heels and used her leg muscles to add momentum.

"Wait a second," Rosie said. She got the blanket and spread it on the ground next to the man. "Roll him onto it," she said.

The girls knelt in the dirt and shoved the man to the center of the blanket. After folding the blanket across him, Rosie took hold of the two corners by his head, and Kayo grasped the two corners by his feet. They faced the forest with the blanket edges across their shoulders and dragged the man behind them.

"I'm not sure why we're working so hard to

save him," Kayo said. "If he had caught us, we don't know what he planned to do."

"He might have killed us," Rosie said.

But both girls kept pulling the man toward safety.

"He's a creep," Rosie said.

"He's still a person," Kayo said. "He's alive."

"We can't let him burn to death," Rosie said.

A spark leaped across the clearing and landed behind them as they worked. A twig caught fire, and then a larger branch. Tongues of fire licked at their shoes.

When the man was ten feet beyond the farthest patch of fire, the girls rolled him off the blanket and left him lying at the edge of the woods.

"The fire got ahead of us while we were moving him," Rosie said. She whacked the blanket up and down again, beating out the flames. She blinked rapidly, trying to wash the smoke out of her eyes.

"Maybe we should run for it," Kayo said. "We may never get the fire under control. Maybe we should get away while we can."

Rosie watched a patch of weeds ignite near the corner of the log cabin. "If we run away now," she said, "the cabin will burn for sure." She wiped a trickle of sweat from her face before she gathered the blanket in her arms and threw it down along the edge of the cabin, covering the patch of weeds. Quickly, she stamped across the blanket, taking tiny, fast steps.

"I don't really care about the creep's cabin," Kayo said, "but if the cabin burns, the forest will burn, too. We won't be able to stop it once those logs catch."

As she spoke, Kayo grabbed the bucket and headed for the pump. The inside of her nose smarted from the smoke. Kayo tried inhaling through her mouth, but that made her cough. Are we making progress, she wondered, or are we wearing ourselves out in a fight we have no hope of winning?

As Rosie threw the soggy blanket onto a fresh patch of flame, she thought about forest fires she had seen on television. It was horrible to see burning trees toppling like toothpicks.

Her family had driven through a state park once, about a year after a bad forest fire. Rosie had been shocked by the blackened skeletons of trees, and the acres and acres of charred ground where grass and shrubs had once grown. It had looked to her as if nothing, plant or animal, could ever live there again.

I can't let that happen here, Rosie thought. I can't!

She remembered her dad's map, spread on the table last week as they planned this trip. The national park, the national forest, and the wilderness area went for hundreds of miles.

We won't run away from this, Rosie thought. We'll stay and fight the fire as long as we can. If we don't, all those miles and miles of trees will burn.

And Kayo and I will burn with them. We can't outrun a forest fire.

Chapter

12

The sheriff, two deputies, two highway patrol officers, and four people from the volunteer search-and-rescue group met at the gravel road.

The volunteers waited while the officials examined the bicycles.

"There's no sign of any scuffle," one officer said, "and the bike helmets were carefully set together on the ground, not tossed away. My guess is that the kids left the bikes here themselves."

"I agree," the sheriff said. "The girls probably decided to hike up the small road, and they hid the bikes behind the bushes to prevent them from being stolen by a passing motorist."

"In that case," said a young woman volunteer, "let's take my all-terrain vehicle up to the end of this road, and then, if we haven't found them, we'll fan out on foot and work our way back down through the woods."

A second volunteer, a man with a ponytail, turned to the sheriff and said, "When the other searchers arrive, please ask them to line up along the highway, five feet apart, on either side of this gravel road, and start working their way up the hill. We'll meet them as we come down."

The four searchers wore hats with lights attached to the front. They could see where they were going and still have their hands free. Each one also had a walkie-talkie clipped to his or her belt.

"I'll call for a canine unit," the sheriff said. "If the girls are on foot, the dog may be able to track them."

"Let's get started," said the man with the ponytail.

The search began.

Rosie heard a low moan and looked at the hermit.

He rubbed the lump on his head, moaned again, and lifted his head.

Rosie couldn't see the expression on his face because he was beyond the glow of the fire, but she could tell he was staring at the flames.

Keeping one eye on the man, Rosie continued to whack at the fire with the blanket.

He sat up, put one hand on the ground, and rolled onto his knees as if to push himself to his feet.

Rosie watched, her muscles tense.

He groaned and lay down again.

Relieved, Rosie continued to smother patches of fire with the blanket. There were fewer burning spots now, and those she saw were small.

"We're gaining on it!" Kayo cried. "Keep going."

Knowing they almost had the fire out gave both girls fresh energy.

Five minutes after the man woke up, Rosie threw the blanket on the last patch of flame. She stamped on the blanket, making sure the fire was smothered.

Kayo rushed around the clump of trees with another bucket of water and stopped. Rosie stood still in the middle of the blanket.

There were no more flames. The fire was completely out.

Without light from the fire, the black night closed its arms around them again.

Rosie dragged the blanket to the big rock and piled it on top. She didn't want a smoldering ember to ignite the blanket.

Kayo crossed the charred ground and stood beside Rosie. Still panting from the exertion, they watched to be sure no new flames leaped out of the dark. A scorched smell, like one hundred slices of burned toast, hung in the air, but they saw no fire.

"We did it," Kayo said. "It's out."

Rosie raised her right hand. Kayo put the bucket on the ground and gave Rosie a high five.

Moaning, the man struggled to his feet.

The girls stiffened.

The shadowy figure lurched toward them.

"I'm too tired to run," Rosie said under her breath.

"So am I."

They stood beside the rock and waited.

The man staggered to the other side of the rock and stopped. Rosie shivered.

"Saved my house," the man said. "Would have burned."

"Yes," Kayo said.

He looked at the remains of his shirt sleeve. "I was on fire," he said. "Shirt was burning." His speech was slightly slurred; it seemed to take a great effort to utter each word.

"Yes," Rosie said. "It was."

"You." He paused. "You put it out."

The girls nodded.

The man looked down at the rock and then looked behind him. "You moved me," he said, sounding astonished. "Fell here." He glanced behind him again. "Not back there."

Kayo and Rosie said nothing.

"Why?"

"We couldn't leave you in the middle of the fire," Kayo said. "The rest of your clothes would have caught fire, the same as your shirt did. You would have burned to death."

"Saved my life."

Kayo wanted to ask the man why he had tried to make her stay here. Rosie wanted to ask if the baby eagle was still alive.

But both girls were afraid to ask any questions. Right now, the man felt grateful; they did not want to say anything that would remind him of his earlier anger.

"Tired," the man said. "So sleepy."

"You should lie down," Rosie suggested. "You had an awful crack on the head when you fell on that rock. You were unconscious for about fifteen minutes."

The man staggered past the rock without looking at the girls again. He entered the cabin, leaving the door open.

Rosie and Kayo followed him to the bottom of the steps and heard the bed creak as he flopped down on it. Soon they heard loud, even breathing.

The girls plopped wearily down on the porch steps.

"Head injuries sometimes make people sleepy," Rosie whispered. "My brother got hit in the head with a baseball once, and the doctor had Mom and Dad wake him up every hour all night long."

"You aren't planning to wake *him* up every hour, are you?" Kayo said, glancing over her shoulder at the cabin door.

"No. I feel a lot safer when he's asleep."

Kayo picked up the slice of bread that Rosie had dropped earlier. "I would trade all of my duplicate baseball cards for a fresh cinnamon roll," she said as she broke the bread in half and handed half to Rosie.

"Only the duplicates?" Rosie said. "What about your Willie Mays card?"

"Never," Kayo said. "Not if I hadn't eaten for a week and all my ribs showed."

"How do you vote?" Rosie said after they ate the bread. "Stay here or move on?"

"There has to be a trail leading away from the cabin," Kayo said, "but it's senseless to keep moving without a light. Let's look for another lantern while he's asleep."

"I didn't see another lantern when I was inside," Rosie said, "but I was in a hurry. I wanted to get out of there before he came back."

"You almost made it."

They stood and stepped inside the cabin.

The man snored evenly.

The girls walked all around the cabin. "I found

some cans of food," Kayo whispered, "but I can't find a can opener."

Rosie examined the shelves beside the door. "Here's a container of kerosene," she said, "and some wooden matches. But I don't see another lantern. He must have only one."

"Maybe we don't need a different lantern," Kayo said. "The one he dropped might work. The glass broke, but the lantern should still burn."

Rosie stuffed a handful of matches in her pocket and grabbed the kerosene container.

The girls went outside and found the lantern on the ground.

Kayo picked it up. "The metal handle is bent," she said, "but I can still use it." Then she added, "The wick is sopping wet; it will never light."

"There should be a way to get fresh wick," Rosie said. She turned a small knob on the side of the lantern, and dry wick emerged from a slot.

Carefully, she poured kerosene into the lantern's base. "Maybe you should put it on the ground while I light it," she said. "It might flare up, and I don't want to scorch your fingers."

"We should keep it away from anything that might burn," Kayo said. "We don't want to start another fire."

Rosie pushed the blanket and the squirrel skin to the ground, and Kayo set the lantern on the big rock. Rosie struck a match on the rock and held the flame to the dry portion of lantern wick.

The match glowed in the dark night, but the wick failed to catch.

"Try again," Kayo said. "Maybe it takes a few minutes for the wick to get soaked with enough kerosene."

Rosie struck another match. This time, the lantern wick caught. A small flame flickered, grew stronger, and then settled into a steady glow.

Rosie held the lantern as the girls circled the cabin, looking for a path.

On the side of the cabin opposite the pump, they found a narrow opening in the brush.

"It isn't exactly well used," Kayo said, "but it looks more like a trail than anything else I've seen."

"Let's find out where it goes," Rosie said.

The path, if that's what it was, curved gently several times but never disappeared.

When they had walked about a mile, Kayo said, "I'm going to blow the whistle again."

"Good idea."

Kayo gave three long blasts on the whistle. After each *tweet*, the girls stood still and listened, hoping to hear voices. The woods remained silent.

Several times, they paused and looked carefully at the undergrowth to see which way to go.

"If this is really a path," Rosie said, "it hasn't been used for a long time."

They stopped every five minutes and blew the whistle again.

Shortly after the fifth whistle blow, a tangle of prickly blackberry bushes blocked their way.

"We can't go through those," Kayo said.

The girls circled the blackberry patch and looked for the path on the other side. They saw only a sea of sword ferns; the path had ended.

"Which way do you think we should go?" Rosie asked. She held the lantern to their right and then to their left.

"The ground slants downhill a little that way," Kayo said, pointing right. "Let's go that direction."

"Blow the whistle again," Rosie said.

Kayo did.

"I'm glad your mom insisted that we bring the whistle," Kayo said. "Every time I blow it, my hopes go up."

"Mine, too. I thought she was being overprotective, but she was smart."

Half an hour after they left the blackberry patch behind, the moon shone through an opening in the trees and spotlighted one of the stones that Kayo had put on a tree branch.

The girls' spirits soared at the sight.

"We aren't going farther into the woods," Kayo said. "We're headed back the way we came earlier."

"If we don't find the gravel road," Rosie said, "we might still be close enough to it that searchers will hear us."

"*If* they follow the gravel road," Kayo said. "I wonder how long it will take them to find our bikes."

"I wish we hadn't hidden them so carefully."

Kayo blew the whistle again.

A faraway voice responded, "Hello! I hear you!"

The girls stared at each other for a second as they realized what they had heard.

"Yes!" Kayo cried. She clenched her fists and held them above her head, the way she always did when she pitched the final out in a winning baseball game.

Tears of relief glistened in Rosie's eyes. She grinned at Kayo.

"Don't move!" the voice yelled. "Stay where you are and make noise. I'll come to you."

Kayo blew the whistle. *Tweet! Tweet! Tweet!* Over and over again, she took deep breaths and blew as hard as she could.

When Kayo was winded, Rosie shouted, "This way! Here we are! Come this way!"

"I hear you!" the voice called. "Keep making noise. I'm coming." The voice got closer, but it took several minutes of whistle blowing and shouting before the girls glimpsed a light approaching.

Kayo and Rosie ran toward the light, waving their arms and shrieking, "Here we are! This way!"

The search-and-rescue man with the ponytail crashed through the underbrush. When his light hit the girls, he smiled broadly. "Rosie Saunders and Kayo Benton?" he asked.

"Yes!" Rosie cried. "You found us!"

"We are so glad to see you," Kayo said.

"Are you all right?" he asked.

"We're fine, now that you're here," Rosie said.

"Do you have anything to eat?" Kayo asked.

The man laughed. He spoke into his walkie-talkie, reporting that the girls were safe. Then he removed his backpack and opened it.

"I'm Bill Dayton," he said as he handed each girl a box of raisins. "I'm glad to see you, too."

Chapter

13

"Where are we?" Rosie asked. "How far did we walk?"

Bill Dayton consulted a compass and a topography map. "We're not far from Sky Creek, a little over two miles north of Highway 20." He repeated that location into the walkie-talkie.

"Two miles!" Kayo said. "Is that all?"

"We started out riding our bikes on Highway 20," Rosie said, "but I feel as if we hiked at least fifty miles."

"We're about twelve miles from where you left your bikes," Bill said as he took two small apple juice containers from his backpack and gave one to each girl. "But you probably didn't go in a straight line."

"That's for sure," Rosie said.

"We made a complete circle once," Kayo said,

"and ended up at a stump we had already passed."

"So you actually covered a lot more than twelve miles. You're lucky you didn't encounter a black bear. There are lots of them around here."

"We saw a grizzly bear," Kayo said.

"Then you're lucky you're here to tell about it. Why did you go off into the woods like that? Didn't you know it's dangerous?"

"We saw a man steal a baby bald eagle out of its nest," Rosie said.

Anger flashed across their rescuer's face. "Where?" he said. "How did he get to the nest?"

"He climbed a cliff," Kayo said. "The nest was wedged in the rocks near the top of the cliff."

"Are you certain it was a bald eagle?" Bill asked.

"Positive. Two adult eagles flew all around him while he did it. They were screaming and trying to get their baby back."

"We tried to follow the man," Kayo said, "and that's when we got lost."

"We found the man's house," Rosie said.

"It's a little cabin in the woods," Kayo said.

"He lives here? In the national park?"

"Yes," Kayo said.

"He's a taxidermist," Rosie said. "He has stuffed eagles and a falcon and a spotted owl and lots of other stuffed birds. He saw us and chased us and tried to make us stay there."

"The park rangers need to hear this," Bill said. "I don't think it is legal to live on federal property, and it's against the law to hunt eagles and spotted owls anywhere." He held out his hand for the empty juice containers and raisin boxes and put them in his backpack. "Do you think you can walk for another two miles?"

"We'll make it," Kayo said.

"That open lantern flame makes me nervous," Bill said. "I'm going to put it out; you can follow my light."

Rosie handed him the lantern.

He turned the knob on the lantern and extinguished the flame.

"The lantern already started one fire," Rosie said.

"In the woods?"

"Yes," Rosie said.

"Where?" Bill said, reaching for his walkie-talkie.

"We put it out," Kayo said.

Bill raised his eyebrows. "A grizzly bear and a forest fire," he said. "I want to hear the details, but I can wait until we get back. Let's go."

The weary girls followed Bill out of the woods to Highway 20. A highway patrol car, alerted by Bill's walkie-talkie directions, cruised slowly back and forth on that section of road, watching for them. As the trio emerged from the trees, the patrol car drove up, ready to drive them to the motor home.

Rosie and Kayo got in the back seat of the patrol car; Bill sat in front.

"They found a man living in the woods," Bill told the officer as the car started down the highway.

"He needs a doctor," Rosie said. "He fell and hit his head on a rock and was unconscious for a while. Also, his arm got burned in the fire."

The officer looked at Bill in alarm. "Fire?" he said. "What fire? Has it been reported?"

"The girls put it out," Bill said.

The surprised officer glanced over his shoulder at Rosie and Kayo. They smiled.

Parked cars lined the road on both sides of the motor home—highway patrol cars, a van from a radio station, cars belonging to the search-and-rescue volunteers, Sheriff's Department vehicles, and cars that said "U.S. Forest Service" on the side. Spotlights from the patrol cars illuminated the entire scene.

Mr. and Mrs. Saunders waited in front of the motor home. Bone Breath stood on the front seat with his paws on the dashboard, barking loudly.

Rosie and Kayo explained everything they had seen and done, and answered dozens of questions.

They had to repeat their story more than once because the searchers who had spread out through the forest returned at different times.

When they got to the part about the grizzly bear, a forest ranger said, "Black bears are common here, but there are only about twenty known grizzlies in this area. Sightings are rare."

"Leave it to Rosie and Kayo to find one of them," Mr. Saunders muttered.

The girls estimated that they had walked a mile and a half from when they left the cabin to where Bill found them. That guess, together with Bill's information about their location when he found the girls, enabled the forest rangers to figure out approximately where the log cabin was.

A ranger, a medic with a stretcher, and two sheriff's deputies headed in that direction. A search helicopter whirred loudly overhead, its bright light aimed at the forest below it.

"Thank you all for helping to find us," Rosie said.

"We're sorry we caused so much trouble," Kayo said.

"We're going to spend the night at Rockport State Park," Mr. Saunders told the sheriff. "When you find that man, we'd like to know who he is and what happens to him next."

"We'll keep you informed," the sheriff promised.

The motor home pulled away, with Rosie and Kayo waving at their rescuers.

"As soon as we get to camp," Mrs. Saunders said, "you girls need showers. Then I'll put antiseptic on all those scratches."

"We want to eat first," Rosie said. "We're starving."

"And exhausted," Kayo said. "I plan to sleep for a week."

The girls each ate a bowl of granola as soon as the motor home stopped.

Rosie put her spoon down and rubbed her arm. "Do we have anything to stop itching?" she asked. "I have a zillion mosquito bites."

It was nearly dawn before they were finally settled in their sleeping bags. When the sheriff knocked on the motor home door at eight o'clock, Rosie and Kayo were still sound asleep. Bone Breath's barking woke them.

Mr. and Mrs. Saunders, who were already dressed, invited the sheriff to have coffee and a blueberry muffin with them at the picnic table. Rosie and Kayo dressed quickly and hurried outside to hear the sheriff tell what had happened. Bone Breath, who was leashed to the picnic table, sat at the sheriff's feet, hoping some crumbs might drop.

"The man was asleep in the cabin when we got there," the sheriff said. "He seemed shocked to see us, but he came with us without a struggle. We had him checked by a doctor, who recommended that he be hospitalized for a day or two. He has second-degree burns on one arm and a concussion. He also has quite a history."

The sheriff took a bite of muffin, and the others waited for him to continue.

Drool dripped off Bone Breath's beard, forming a small puddle on the concrete under the picnic table. He kept his eyes on the muffin.

"His name is Woodrow Dunn," the sheriff said, "and he was declared legally dead five years ago."

Rosie and Kayo looked at each other with wide eyes.

"Mr. Dunn was a carpenter in Colorado," the sheriff said. "He was also a mountain climber and avid hunter whose hobby was taxidermy. Apparently, he was always a loner who preferred to work by himself. When his wife and daughter were killed in a car wreck, Mr. Dunn fell apart. He never recovered from the tragedy."

As Rosie listened, she looked around at the ancient trees in the state park. Moss hung from branches, swaying gently in the breeze.

The sheriff continued. "One day, about a month after the accident, Mr. Dunn packed up his taxidermy supplies, put a suicide note on the dashboard of his truck, and parked beside a high bridge over the Colorado River."

"But he didn't jump," Rosie said.

"No. He walked out onto the bridge and laid a shirt, shoes, and a pair of pants on the edge of the bridge. His wallet was in the pants pocket; it contained his driver's license. But he never jumped."

"Who was he trying to fool?" Mrs. Saunders asked.

"He sounds completely crazy," Mr. Saunders said.

"Even though no body was ever found in the river," the sheriff continued, "it was assumed that he had jumped off the bridge and drowned. Instead, he walked on across the bridge and hitched a ride to the West Coast. He hiked into the North Cascades National Park and built the cabin and furniture himself, and he's been there ever since."

"Weird," Kayo said.

"His only family, two sisters, thought he was dead; it was quite a shock this morning when they learned that he isn't."

"How did he manage, all alone like that?" Mrs. Saunders asked.

"He must have had some cash on him when he left home," Rosie said, "because he bought the lantern and blankets and tools to dig the well."

"He isn't completely self-sufficient," the sheriff replied. "He has a deal with a man from Seattle, someone Mr. Dunn knew in high school, who provides basic necessities. The man comes three times a year, bringing canned beans, flour, coffee, and other supplies. In exchange, he takes the birds that Mr. Dunn stuffs and sells them."

"Do you know who that man is?" Kayo asked.

"Mr. Dunn wouldn't tell, but we found an old business card with a Seattle address tacked on one wall of the cabin. The Seattle police are contacting that person this morning."

"Why didn't Mr. Dunn want us to leave?" Rosie asked. "What was he planning to do if he had caught us?"

The sheriff sipped his coffee and sighed. "Mr. Dunn was never the most stable person," he said, "and so many years of solitude and grief took a toll on his mental health. He panicked when he saw you, which made his mind even worse. If he had caught you, he planned to keep you in the cabin until his friend came."

"That doesn't make sense," Kayo said. "We told him searchers would find us."

The sheriff shrugged and handed his last bite of muffin to Bone Breath, who swallowed it whole. "Like I said, Mr. Dunn doesn't think too clearly anymore. Probably he was already slipping into mental illness when he faked his own death, and he's become more eccentric every year since."

"Poor soul," Mrs. Saunders said. "Perhaps he'll get help now."

"His sisters have already scheduled a mental evaluation."

"When you searched the cabin," Rosie said, "did you find the eaglet that he stole yesterday?"

"We found its body," the sheriff said grimly.

Tears pooled in Rosie's eyes. Kayo dug the toe of her shoe in the dirt.

"You tried to save it," Mrs. Saunders said softly. "You did your best."

"If Mr. Dunn had not been caught," the sheriff said, "he might have gone back today for the second eaglet."

"He would have killed birds for many more years," Mr. Saunders said.

"Your Care Club project has saved the lives of countless birds," Mrs. Saunders said.

The sheriff's beeper went off, and he excused himself to make a call from his car. When he returned, he said, "The Seattle police located Mr. Dunn's accomplice. He admitted selling the birds, but he claims he didn't know any of them were taken illegally. He said he was merely helping an old friend survive."

"A likely story," Mr. Saunders said.

Bone Breath wagged his tail and licked the sheriff's shoe.

As the sheriff drove away, Mr. Saunders said,

"Let's pack up and head home. My nerves are shot."

"We can't go home yet," Rosie said. "I need more information on eagles so I can write my report. Mrs. Cushman said extra credit reports have to be at least two pages long."

Mr. Saunders rolled his eyes.

Mrs. Saunders said, "You can surely write two pages about what happened last night. There's enough material for a whole book."

Rosie smiled, knowing her mother was right. "I thought of a good title for my report," she said. "I'm going to call it *Screaming Eagles*."

"*Screaming Parents* would be more accurate," said Mr. Saunders.

About the Author

Peg Kehret's popular novels for young people are regularly nominated for state awards. She has received the Young Hoosier Award, the Golden Sower Award, the Iowa Children's Choice Award, the Sequoyah Award, the Celebrate Literacy Award, the Pacific Northwest Young Reader's Choice Award, the Maud Hart Lovelace Award, and the New Mexico Land of Enchantment Award. She lives with her husband, Carl, and their animal friends in Washington State, where she is a volunteer at The Humane Society and SPCA. Her two grown children and four grandchildren live in Washington, too.

Peg's Minstrel titles include *Nightmare Mountain; Sisters, Long Ago; Cages; Terror at the Zoo; Horror at the Haunted House;* and the *Frightmares*™ series.

R·L·STINE'S

GHOSTS of FEAR STREET®

1 HIDE AND SHRIEK
52941-2/$3.99

2 WHO'S BEEN SLEEPING IN MY GRAVE?
52942-0/$3.99

3 THE ATTACK OF THE AQUA APES
52943-9/$3.99

4 NIGHTMARE IN 3-D
52944-7/$3.99

5 STAY AWAY FROM THE TREEHOUSE
52944-7/$3.99

6 EYE OF THE FORTUNETELLER
52946-3/$3.99

7 FRIGHT KNIGHT
52947-1/$3.99

8 THE OOZE
52948-X/$3.99

Available from Minstrel® Books
Published by Pocket Books

POCKET
BOOKS